Carnival of Horror

Undertaker Books

Undertaker Books

UNDERTAKER BOOKS
www.undertakerbooks.com

Contents

INTRODUCTION

Folks, I am tired.

Carnival of Horror was our sixth open-anthology call since we launched Undertaker Books in March 2024. We received over 200 submissions to the call, all of them read by yours truly. Across all six of our calls, we received over 600 submissions, again, all read by yours truly.Did I mention I'm tired?

It's a good tired—I love editing anthologies. But I'm ready for a break.

And leaving readers with *Carnival of Horror* as our most recent anthology for a few months is an exciting prospect.

Narrowing the massive volume of submissions down to a final ten was not an easy task. I missed being able to dump some of the work off on our much-missed anthology assistant, Avery Lewis (like this introduction. I don't enjoy writing introductions). In the end, after numerous challenging decisions, I came up with a table of contents.

We've got some familiar faces in this anthology. Ann O'Mara Heyward makes her second appearance in an Undertaker Books anthology (her story "The Monster Maker" was included in our first anthology, *Mortuary Edition*). Chloe York and Amanda M. Blake celebrate their second selections but first publications (both have stories in *High Seas Edition* you'll see later this year). And, as usual, one of my own stories will be making an appearance.

In addition to our old friends, we also have some new faces: T.S. Weaver, Jamie Churchman, and S.E. Howard are Americans making their Undertaker debuts. Finally, we have three international authors: Leonardo Lamanna from Italy, Marie McWilliams from Northern Ireland, and Lauren Mills from Australia.

This anthology features stories that soar and scream, that bring consequences and freedom. It is, in my own opinion, one of the best anthologies we've put together, and I'm excited to share it with you.

D.L. Winchester

Newport, TN

2/26/25

CARNIVAL OF HORROR

AN UNDERTAKER BOOKS ANTHOLOGY

THE FLOSS WAGON

D.L. WINCHESTER

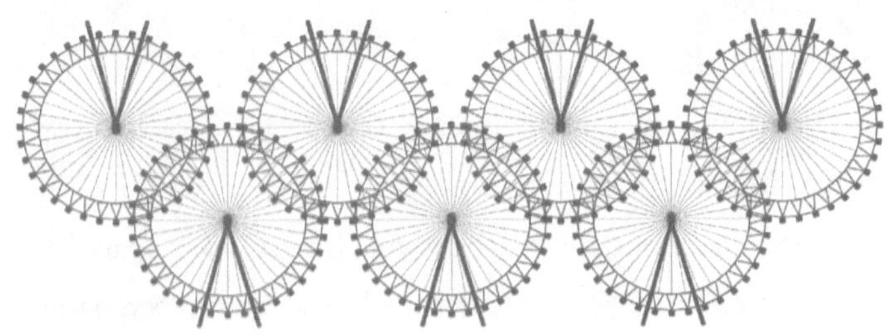

THE TALL, GAUNT MAN in an orange coat pushed a pink and blue floss wagon down the carnival's midway. "Get your cotton candy! Cotton candy, right here, folks!"

His voice joined the chorus around him: barkers working to bring marks to their games, their calls echoing over the laughter of children and the distant sounds of whirling rides.

He sold a spool of cotton candy to a young couple, then another to an older gentleman, before the soft whimpering coming from inside the floss wagon became too much.

The man cracked a small door under the cart's handle. "Keep cranking, boy," he hissed. "Wouldn't want the monsters to get you."

"I'm tired, mister," came the reply. "I don't know how much longer I can crank."

Damn kids. Years ago, you could promise a kid a cotton candy spool and they'd crank for hours, or even days. Now, after thirty minutes they were worn out and wanted to go find their mommies.

"Keep cranking," he hissed.

"My arms hurt!"

"Fine." Slipping the cart behind the ring toss, he reached down and opened the door all the way.

Inside, nestled among the gears and machinery, was a space barely big enough for a small child. A crank attached to gears connected to the floss bowl, with just enough room for the child to rotate the device.

The boy climbed out, and the man handed him a pink cloud of cotton candy on a paper stick.

The kid almost dropped it, but as soon as he took the first bite, his exhaustion disappeared and a smile crossed his face.

"Thanks, mister," he said, his blue eyes sparkling as he ran off to join the crowd on the midway.

"Switching out again, Craig?" a carny sneaking a smoke asked.

"Kids ain't got the stamina anymore." The old machine was a pain in the ass, but that touch of salt from the evaporated sweat made his cotton candy the best around.

"Shit, years ago, we had a kid in the cart for almost a month. Didn't cry or nothing." The carny took a last drag on his smoke. "No one came looking for him, either. 'Course, after all that time in the cart, we had us a top-notch hunchback." He tossed the butt to the ground and wandered off.

As Craig turned to get back to the midway, he saw a boy wandering down the alley between the games. He was maybe five, small and thin, the perfect size for the floss wagon.

"Are you lost, kid?" Craig asked.

The boy nodded.

"Looking for your mama?"

He nodded again.

Craig grinned. "Don't worry, kid. I'll help you find your mama. But while we look, how would you like to earn a spool of cotton candy?"

"Cotton candy!" Craig steered the floss cart between the ferris wheel and the tilt-a-whirl. "Get your cotton candy!"

"Hey, mister!" A girl jerked on the tail of his coat, and Craig turned to glare at her.

No one touched the cotton candy man.

She ignored his glare. "My little brother, Liam, is lost. Have you seen him?"

"Naw. You need to talk to security." He looked around for one of the officers, their neon yellow shirts making them stand out in the crowd.

She grabbed his coat again. "I'm talking to you, mister."

"What? Get out of here, kid!" Craig pushed the cart away. "Get your cotton candy!"

Another hard yank on his sleeve.

"What the hell do you want, girl?"

"My brother! His name is Liam and I know he's inside your little cart!"

"You're dreaming. I don't have anyone in my cart!" He pushed the floss wagon away, looking for a place to get rid of the evidence.

"You put him in there!" The girl insisted. "I have it on video!"

Craig whipped around. "What did you say?"

She held up her phone, the screen showing the little boy climbing into his floss wagon.

"What the fuck is this?"

She grinned. "I want my brother, and the cotton candy you promised him."

Craig shook his head. Maybe it was time to retire the old cart. Everyone had a damn camera these days. Phones were ruining everything. "Fine." He steered the wagon behind one of the motor homes that housed the carnys. Craig opened the door, and Liam climbed out, looking dazed.

"What's wrong with him?" the girl asked.

Craig smiled. "The magic still has him. He won't be okay until he eats some cotton candy."

"Then give him some."

"Not yet," Craig said. "I don't want him to remember this."

It was a tight squeeze, but he managed to wedge the girl into the floss wagon. "Turn the crank, or the monsters will get you," he hissed as he closed the door.

Reaching into the spinner bowl, he assembled a cloud of cotton candy and handed it to Liam.

He took a bite, and a smile returned to his face. "Thanks for the help, Mister. I guess we didn't find my mom."

"No." Craig grinned. "Maybe you should check with security."

The boy nodded, then looked at the floss wagon. It was making a weird grinding sound, like it might come apart. "I think your machine's gonna break."

"Just needs some oil," Craig assured him, then watched as Liam turned and ran off toward the midway.

A scream came from inside the floss wagon.

Craig cracked the door and leaned over. "Turn the crank, my dear," he hissed. "Turn the crank and the monsters will leave you alone."

On the wagon, the bowl began to spin as Craig headed back toward the midway. "Cotton candy!" he called. "Get your cotton candy here!"

FLESH PUPPETS

LEONARDO LAMANNA

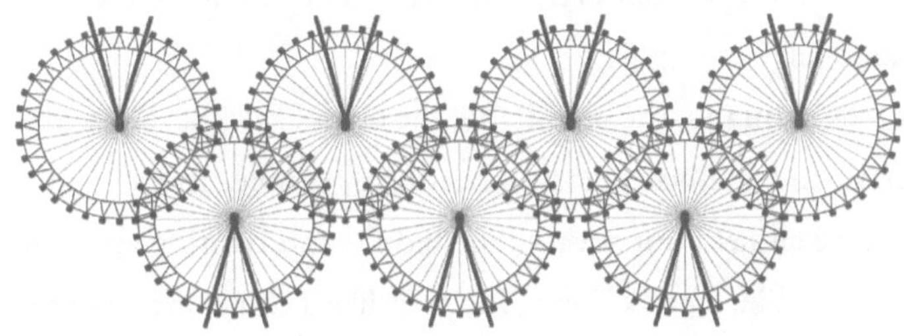

ONCE A YEAR, THE Circus journeys across the Badlands, like the sun crawling through a polluted sky, never lingering too long in one place. It has always been this way, for as long as anyone can remember.

Tonight is special for the whole village—but for me, it's even more so.

I'm here for Miranda. My dream. My love. Miranda, whose eyes are diamonds in the darkness. Miranda, whose breasts are low hills lit by the glow of dawn. Miranda, my childhood companion, my youthful passion, the one I whispered sweet words to when we lay together among the trash, dreaming beneath the full moon.

"One day, I'll go with them," she used to say. "I'll be one of them, Gregor. One of those magnificent puppets, and I'll soar high, far away from here. Then, death will never touch me again."

I would stroke her face, marred by tumors, and lose myself in the phosphorescent glow of her eyes.

"Yes, you will, Miranda," I'd whisper, my stomach knotting with dread. "You can do it—you just need a little more practice..."

"There's no more time, Gregor," she would say, clutching my hand tighter. "It's this year or never. When the Circus comes to the village, I'll face the Trial."

Oh, the pain! Oh, the blood! Oh, the terror! But she did it. She faced the Trial, and she was graceful, beautiful, supple, and strong. When she fell, we all held our breath. She didn't stop twisting and spinning, plummeting like a hawk diving for prey, like a comet crashing to earth, like a vortex of light. When she hit the ground in a cloud of crimson dust, the crowd erupted in adoration.

The Master rose from his throne—a pale giant with black, hollow eyes devoid of light. Slowly, he approached little Miranda. He knelt by her broken body and placed a soft kiss on her forehead. For a few minutes, he watched her in complete silence while we all strained to hear her ragged breaths. Then, he gathered her in his massive arms, a shattered bird, and carried her away to the Circus to make her one of his puppets.

That night was a grand one for our village.

Miranda returned the following year with the Circus. She was a perfect being now. Her pale skin was smooth and flawless, free of the lumps and sores, and her golden hair shone brighter than it ever had before.

I pushed closer, calling her name, pleading for her to see me, but she didn't. The living puppets soar too high in their endless flights to bother looking down.

Still, I searched for her gaze that night and every night after. Year after year. But it was all in vain.

Miranda was a goddess, and I was just a scrap of flesh, clinging to the bottom of the universe. And yet, I started to wonder if there might be a chance for me too. After all, wasn't Miranda born in the Badlands, same as me?

How many times had I helped her train, improvising obstacle courses between the walls of trash? I had learned much myself in those days—swinging from beams, vaulting over pools of acid, leaping backward from stacks of barrels to the shell of an old car, and landing with perfect poise amidst jagged, twisted scrap metal.

If Miranda had passed the Trial, why couldn't I?

They called me crazy, tried to talk me out of it. For what? To waste away year by year, my organs rotting in the Badlands' poisoned air, just like my father and mother? No, thank you. This will be the last time I stand among the crowd, neck craned, searching for a glimpse of Miranda—a glance that will never come.

Now, I am ready. My training is complete. Tomorrow, I'll face the Trial. My act is spectacular. I told myself: "If you're going to do it, make it unforgettable."

Soon, I'll be with Miranda, up there in the wind and the light.

I woke before dawn, though I'd hardly slept. At times, I drifted into a restless haze, reliving fragments of my past, back when I was just a boy. Miranda was there, of course.

I choked down the usual lumpy gruel for breakfast and searched for a puddle that wasn't too filthy to clean myself.

One must look their best for the Trial. You need the Master to notice you, to fix your face in his mind.

My Trial is set for sunset, as the rules dictate. I spend the rest of the day alone, putting the final touches on the machines I built for my act and trying to focus on the stunts.

Shortly before dusk, I mix together all the substances I've collected over the past year: battery acid brimming with lead and mercury, for concentration; nickel filings scraped from the metal casing of an old van, to sharpen my reflexes; various chemical solvents to quicken my heartbeat. I pour everything into a cup and gulp it down. Finally, I chew on a few adrenal glands I harvested yesterday from a family of ferrets.

I hope training and adrenaline will take care of the rest.

At sunset, I arrive at the Circus. They're waiting for me. I climb the tall structure of wood, metal, and ropes built for the Trial. Step after step, I ascend the endless ladder, higher and higher, to the platform where it all begins.

Now I see him, the Master. He sits on his throne of iron and human bones, two hundred feet below me—immense and unmovable, like a mountain. Beside him stand the automatons, his glorious flesh puppets, divine progeny born of his hands.

From up here, I see the Badlands as I've never seen them before. I take a moment, letting the cold winter wind lash against my face. The Badlands lie beneath me, its hard crust of dust and garbage stretching far and wide. The village, a black cluster of wreckage, is below me. My fellow villagers, bloated, twisted, and limping, stand below me, their heads tilted upward.

Not many are praying for me, I know. Not like they did for Miranda. Even Miranda is beneath me now, with the other puppets. She sits at the Master's feet, his favored creation. She isn't looking at me. She's chatting cheerfully with a friend, like carefree children.

The first trumpet blast pulls me back to reality—the biting wind, the dizzying height, the narrow wooden ledge beneath my feet. It's so small that my toes hang over the edge. Strange birds of indescribable colors circle around me, shrieking harshly.

The second trumpet sounds. The Trial will begin soon. Drums roll. The Master raises an arm. Is he watching me with interest? Or boredom? He's too far away for me to tell.

The Master's arm falls, and the trumpet blares a third time. I bend my knees and leap into the void.

The first part of my act isn't too difficult. After a perfect somersault, I dive toward a bar and grab it with both hands, deftly dodging two bursts of flame from a pair of flamethrowers. They would have incinerated me if I were too slow, but I escape with only a burn on my right shoulder.

Now, I let my body spin around the bar, straight as an arrow—once, twice, three times. This part allows me to catch my breath, though I hope it doesn't seem too obvious. Then, when I'm perfectly aligned above it, I let go, launching myself into the air. I perform a series of flips and twists, all while dodging enormous, razor-sharp blades swinging back and forth from the rigging. They'd slice me to ribbons if I so much as grazed them. I know because I sharpened them myself.

Somersaults have always been my specialty. But twists? Not so much. That's where I make my first mistake. The sharp edge of a metal sheet slices through my left leg, cleanly severing it mid-tibia.

Idiot! Out of the corner of my eye, I see the severed piece of my leg spinning through the air, tumbling down into the crowd below.

I don't care. Focus. That's all that matters. Below me, I spot the tiny wooden platform marked with a black X. Balancing on my remaining leg, I aim to land, keeping the stump parallel to where it should be, as if I were going to finish with a neat, two-footed landing. Pain claws at my throat, almost dragging out a scream, but I manage to stifle it.

Without glancing at the wound, I tighten the tourniquet strapped just below my knee. It's something I prepared for this exact scenario, as I've done with the other straps tied around my thighs, forearms, and biceps. Just a few minutes of survival—that's all I need. A nasty injury like this can drain your blood faster than you think, killing you before you even finish the act. That would be a disaster.

The next part is easier—or so I tell myself. With a graceful motion, I shift into a perfect handstand, walking along two taut steel cables stretched high above the ground. The cables sway, but they're tight enough to provide just the right amount of stability for my trembling arms. My shoulder and back muscles scream with the strain, quivering under the weight. In this position, blood rushes to my head, briefly easing the throbbing agony in the stump of my leg.

Fifteen feet down the line, as planned, a spinning blade whirs to life, grinding along its axis and spewing sparks as it begins to slice through the cables. Steel screeches against steel, the sound grating in my ears as tiny sparks dance across my back.

Are they watching in awe down there? Is the Master impressed by my ingenuity? I can't think about that now. Every ounce of my focus is on reaching the end of the cables before they snap and send me plummeting a hundred and fifty feet onto the concrete below.

The wind picks up—harsh, cold, unpredictable. It hadn't been an issue during rehearsals, which I'd done only thirty feet off the ground. But up here, so close to the sky, the gales sweeping in from the Badlands are fierce.

A gust slams into me, nearly breaking my grip. I clutch the frayed cables tighter, letting the jagged edges dig into my palms. Rusty, splintered steel threads tear into my flesh, but they give me a better hold.

Ignore the pain. Ignore the fire searing your nerves. It'll be over soon. You'll be a god.

I reach the trampoline just as the last threads of cable give way. A jagged shard of steel embedded in my left hand wrenches off my pinky and ring finger as I release the wire.

Sweat and grime sting my eyes, forcing them shut. There might be applause from below—I think I hear it—but it fades quickly. The Master is still watching, though. The automatons chatter amongst themselves, bored. Miranda stretches, rubbing her calves while her friend whispers something in her ear.

Enough distractions. Let's finish this.

The stump below my knee starts to throb again, as blood flows back into my leg, a slave to gravity. All of us bags of rotting flesh, refuse of the Badlands, we are all slaves to gravity. The Master's automatons are not—they live in the air and the wind, just as we worms live in the dark earth. It's a good thing, I think, that the Master is still watching, because now is the time for the grand finale.

The trampoline will launch me skyward, giving me the height I need. After a few flashy flips, I'll use my remaining foot to activate a lever mid-flight. That lever will trigger a series of acid jets—my own invention, cobbled together from salvaged plastic tubing.

There can be no mistakes now. If I time it perfectly— twist, two flips, two more twists—I'll avoid the acid. If not, I'll be doused, melting into a blistered heap of organic sludge as I plummet at fifty miles an hour.

But I won't fail. I've rehearsed every move a thousand times.

I raise my arms to the sky, demanding their attention. Watch me! The drumroll begins anew. The sun sets over the Badlands, a swollen red eye glaring down on the scene.

One. Two. Three. Go.

Two somersaults—flawless. My foot hits the lever, triggering a sharp click. I hear the faint hiss of the acid jets activating.

At the apex of my jump, I prepare for the twist.

But in that split second, I glance down and see Miranda. She's looking back at me, her diamond-colored eyes glinting as she smiles.

That's all it takes.

I lose focus. The twist is a mess—a graceless, spasmodic jerk.

The first spray of acid strikes my side, carving through flesh like a blade. I taste the bitterness of it in my mouth as crimson clouds erupt from my ribs, scattering into the evening air.

The second jet grazes me. The third, the final one, hits me square in the face.

There's heat, then cold. My teeth sink into something—my tongue, a chunk of jaw, who knows?

The impact never comes. Or maybe I just don't feel it.

I've failed. Made a fool of myself. Yet somehow, I'm still thinking. Pain ebbs and flows, a distant tide in the vast ocean of my disintegrating body. Slime doesn't feel pain, I think. I'm becoming slime.

Above me, the sky glows red. Then, movement—a towering figure looms over my remains.

The Master.

He's risen from his throne. For me? What does he want to say? His mouth moves, but no sound reaches me.

There's another face now. Miranda. She's leaning over me, smiling.

"Miranda," I whisper—or think I do. I can't tell if I'm speaking anymore.

Her expression shifts, surprised, uncertain.

"You know my name?" she asks, her voice sharp and clear.

"I'm...Gregor," I murmur.

She shakes her head. "I'm sorry. I don't know you."

"Kids...together...," I try to say.

"Oh, I see," she says. "Maybe we knew each other back when I was still a scrap, like you. But you see, when the Master turned me into one of his automatons, he erased my memory."

I watch her slipping away, swaying and distorting before my eyes—but that's probably because my vision is turning to jelly.

"You... looked at me," I manage to rasp, my voice barely a whisper.

"Oh, that's true. I wasn't interested in your number, though. I looked because my friend pointed out that you have a particularly well-developed hamstring."

"Huh?"

"The muscle on your thigh. It's flexible and strong. And it's almost undamaged from the fall. Lucky for me. Mine's been a bit stiff lately. But the Master knows how to replace it. We just needed a suitable donor."

"Ha... hamstr..." I try to say, but my words collapse into a gurgle of blood and spit.

"Thanks, whoever you are. What was your name again? Oh, well, it doesn't matter. You never would have passed the Trial with that silly number of yours. But at least you'll be useful in another way."

I see the Master's shape hovering above me, just a dark blur now. I feel hands grabbing me. Then a hum, the sound of things snapping and crumbling inside me.

Somehow, I feel at peace.

Somehow, I'll always be with Miranda, drifting among the stars and the light.

KIDDIE TOWN

JAMIE CHURCHMAN

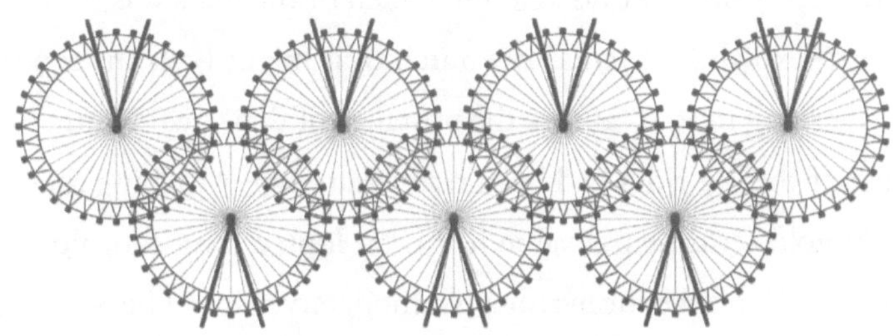

"Oh, man, everything's *gone*," Mindy said, surveying the land in front of her.

Trent dropped down off the chain-link fence next to Mindy and turned his phone's flashlight on. The grounds in front of them were mostly barren, with the occasional metal track poking out of the earth like the skeleton of some dismembered steel beast. Realizing that the full moon illuminated more than his flashlight, Trent shut it off.

"They left the Scare Shack standing, but God knows if anything is still inside. And last I heard, Kiddie Town is completely untouched."

The fence rattled as Ashley and Jason climbed over to join them. "You can still see some of the wooden supports for the old roller coaster," Jason said.

"The ones that didn't burn up in the last fire. Or the fire before that." Ashley paused for a second. "Or the fire before *that*."

The two couples made their way deeper into the gutted amusement park. Moonlight glinted off broken glass and discarded beer cans, accumulated over the last twenty years, starting the day Joyland had shut its gates forever. Mindy wondered how much of the mess was the detritus of teenage expeditions, and how much of it might be from adults like them, sneaking in to recapture the nostalgia of their own youth.

Most of the big rides had been razed years ago. Anything that could possibly hold sentimental value had been looted long ago, along with anything that could conceivably hold monetary value. The Scare Shack, once the ultimate test of younger siblings' and cowardly friends' bravery, was now nothing more than a dilapidated, graffiti-covered wooden building with a broken track hanging down from the second story. The sign had long since been stolen, a tell-tale patch of wood darker than the surrounding boards showing where it had once been.

The group wound around the disappointing husk of the Scare Shack and stopped. Beyond it lay Kiddie Town. As the name suggested, this was the area of the amusement park dedicated to the gentle rides for children. Baby rides, as they'd all scornfully referred to them back when they were teenagers. Mindy had moved to town when she was thirteen and thus had never ridden any of the kiddie rides, but the other three were lifelong residents with fond memories of Kiddie Town.

"Oh my God," Ashley said, running forward and hopping the waist-high gate to the rides area. Flakes of rust rained down at her touch. She wiped her hand on her jeans. "Look, it's the Kiddie Town Train!"

Jason followed her, frowning at the orange rust stains on his hands and jeans. "This whole place is tetanus waiting to happen. Don't cut yourselves on anything."

Mindy carefully climbed over the fence, trying to avoid the most rusted places. It was impossible; the entire fence was coated in it, the gate long since immobile from the stuff. The train Ashley had pointed out was directly in front of them. Chest-high train cars had once taken little kids in a circle around Kiddie Town, a miniature version of the train that had taken riders on a trek around the perimeter of Joyland.

The train cars were now rusted, the paint faded and chipped. In fact, as Mindy looked around, she saw that everything in Kiddie Town was rusted and faded. Trent may have been right about the area being untouched by bulldozers, but time and the elements hadn't been as considerate.

Trent walked to the next ride, a baby roller coaster. Cars shaped like generic cartoon animals followed a circular track with hills that barely reached his knees. "This must have been absolutely terrifying for the three-year-olds."

"I'm pretty sure I remember you peeing your pants," Jason said.

"Well, yeah. I was three."

Ashley wove her way past the kiddie coaster and put a hand on one of the helicopter ride's animal-shaped cars. The elephant was faded to a grungy gray, the painted eyes completely chipped away, leaving only blank white spaces. "Aw, poor dollar store Dumbo."

"Guys, why hasn't anything in here been looted or destroyed?" Mindy asked, looking around again. Surely some destructive teenagers out for a good time should have taken a baseball bat to the fiberglass characters by now. Swear words and faux-Satanic graffiti should have been spray-painted on every available surface.

"Reverence for the innocence of childhood?" Ashley suggested, shrugging.

"Doubt it," Jason muttered.

Mindy shook her head and continued on the trail past the mini coaster. To her right was a tiny carousel, barely bigger than the coin operated ones that had been outside every grocery store when she'd been small.

To her left was a line of scaled-down carnival game booths, meant to emulate the midway, but for the little ones. Directly in front of her was a remarkably well-maintained concrete path leading to a fifteen-foot-tall structure made to look like a boot.

"Oh my God, The Old Woman Who Lived in a Shoe's shoe!" Ashley squealed, running past her.

"Watch out," Jason called after her. "There might be a pack of rabid raccoons living in there now."

"A *gaze* of rabid raccoons," Mindy corrected absently, staring at The Old Woman's Shoe. There was a pass-through arch in the side, and a door set into one side of the arch, leading into the heel of the boot. Hanging out over the toes was a balcony. Small windows dotted the heel and ankle, allowing glimpses of a staircase inside.

"I forgot this was back here," Trent said. He looked at Mindy. "It's really tiny inside. I almost got stuck on the staircase when I was seven."

Mindy tilted her head, taking in the brown boot with its yellow trim. A white A-frame roof topped the structure, clean and shining in the moonlight. She frowned and looked around her at the rest of the rides, tired and faded, mere ghosts of their former bright and cheery selves. "Why isn't this one faded like all the rest? It looks brand new."

At the archway, Ashley had ducked down to try the door, frowning when she tried to turn the knob. "Hey, it's locked! I didn't even know it *had* a lock."

"Maybe it's rusted shut," Jason called, jogging up to join her.

"No, there's no rust anywhere."

"Like I said," Mindy started, reluctantly walking closer to the giant shoe, "it looks like it was installed yesterday."

Trent inspected it, furrowing his brow. "Super weird. I don't even think it looked this good when we were kids."

Jason looked at them and shrugged, then turned back to Ashley. "Maybe you should knock. It *is* the polite thing to do."

"Don't," Mindy said, even as Ashley's knuckles hit the wood. The others gave her a strange look. She shook her head in reply. She couldn't explain it, but she'd been hit by an overwhelming sense of dread as soon as Ashley had crouched down to enter the archway.

Ashley peered through the tiny window in the door, then ducked back out of the arch and shrugged, raising her arms dramatically. "I guess no one's home."

"Probably a good thing," Trent said. "Remember at the end of the nursery rhyme the old lady whips the shit out of the kids."

Ashley frowned and looked over her shoulder at the shoe. "You know, it's kinda messed up they put that here, then."

Mindy let out a breath as everyone seemed finished inspecting the Old Woman's Shoe. They had turned toward the tiny midway when she caught motion from the corner of her eye. She turned back to the Shoe and squinted, trying to figure out what she'd seen. It had been quick, like the sun reflecting off a ripple in a pond. She glanced up at the full moon, still casting its silvery light across Kiddie Town.

"Mindy? What's wrong?" Ashley asked, cocking her head.

"Nothing." She forced a small laugh. "I spooked myself, that's all. Thought I saw something moving inside the Shoe, but it must have been a reflection in one of the windows."

Ashley froze. "There's no glass in those windows. They're just empty frames."

Mindy swallowed and looked back at the Shoe. A dark shape moved within one of the lower windows. Higher, something crouched on the balcony, hidden in shadow. She shivered as the crouched mass moved toward the balcony's railing, moonlight catching and reflecting light from two small spots in the shadows.

Eyes.

Ashley had seen it, too. She grabbed Mindy's arm and pulled her toward the guys, who had stopped in front of the mini midway. "Jason, Trent," she hissed. "We've gotta go."

Trent didn't pick up on the urgency in her voice. "Hey, should we look for the Ring Toss rings back there?"

"Sure, if you like spiders," Jason said.

"Guys, seriously, there's something in the Old Woman's Shoe," Ashley told them.

"Well yeah, like a shit ton of children, right?" Trent grinned.

"No, Trent," Mindy said. "Something else. We need to leave right now."

"Raccoons," Jason said.

Although they were now twenty yards away from the Shoe, the sound of creaking hinges reached them clearly. A soft thump followed, and then another. The whisper-soft sound of footsteps shuffling along the concrete around the Shoe came after that.

"Not raccoons," Ashley whispered.

Dark figures, vaguely child-shaped, were slowly emerging from the Shoe. Some slunk out from the door; others slid off the balcony. Silver eyes shone in the moonlight as the shadowy children turned toward Mindy's group.

"Oh, God," Trent murmured.

"Let's go. Let's go let's go let's go," Ashley breathed, grabbing Jason's arm and turning toward the exit.

Trent reached out to take Mindy's hand. She dreaded turning her back to the dark figures; felt their eyes boring into her as the group not-quite-ran away from the Old Woman's Shoe.

They didn't get far before the sound of a train whistle reached them. It sounded faint, not like it was coming from far away, but like it had no strength behind it. Ashley stopped in her tracks, pulling Jason to a halt beside her.

"Is that the Kiddie Town Train?" she asked, her voice a mixture of horror and incredulity.

"It can't be," Trent said, but Mindy didn't think he sounded very confident. "There's no power to the park, none of the rides work."

As he finished speaking, the string lights draped around the perimeter of Kiddie Town began to glow dimly. Somewhere behind them, the tiny carousel started up its tinny music. The metal creaked and squealed as the carousel revolved, the fairytale creatures slowly rising and falling on their steel poles.

The shadow children were advancing now, some shuffling, others slithering along the ground. They were cloaked in darkness that seemed to move, to writhe around them. It hurt Mindy's eyes to look at them. It hurt her *brain* to try to comprehend what she was seeing.

"It's been so long," one of them said, and the voice surrounded them, as if it came from the park itself.

"Run," Jason whispered, and they took off, weaving around the kids' rides that were creaking and squealing in their weak attempts to come back to life.

They weren't even halfway back to the Kiddie Town entrance when Trent tripped over something unseen in the dark and went sprawling. He leapt to his feet and leaned against the helicopter ride's faux Dumbo car. Blood dripped from a gash on his forearm. The lights around them pulsed brighter, and he stumbled away from the ride as it began to move.

Mindy stared at the elephant car Trent's blood had touched. Were the colors growing brighter on the fiberglass animal? She thought they were, and shivered at the implication.

"Come *on*!" Ashley yelled over her shoulder, racing toward the kiddie coaster. In the split second she wasn't looking in front of her, her foot snagged on one of the tracks. She hit the ground on her elbows and stomach, releasing a harsh grunt.

Jason helped her to her feet, his hand coming away smeared with blood after grabbing her arm. "Tetanus," he muttered breathlessly. "Tetanus and . . . and *creatures*."

"We'll get tetanus shots," Mindy said, coming up behind him and Ashley and putting her hands on their backs to steer them through the center of the kiddie coaster area. "No idea what we're supposed to do about the creatures, though."

Behind them, the shadowy figures crept their way. Even in the brightening light, the shadows remained around them, and Mindy could no more make out what they were than she could when she'd first glimpsed them in the Old Woman's Shoe. As she turned back to the group, the lights on the kiddie coaster came on, and the chain pulleys within the tracks rattled to life. A second later, the coaster itself came flying around the track at them. Mindy pulled Ashley back in time to avoid a collision, but the lead car slammed into Jason's side, knocking him to the ground at Mindy's feet. His jeans were torn, and blood dribbled from his exposed thigh.

"Dammit, would you all stop bleeding on everything in here!" Mindy balled her fists up, closed her eyes, and took a deep breath. When she opened her eyes, her friends were staring at her, and the shadowy children had stopped advancing, forming a semi-circle just outside the coaster track.

"You seek to destroy us." Once again, the voice sounded as though it came from all around them.

"No, we don't!" Mindy shouted. "We didn't come here to loot or destroy anything! We had good times here as kids! We just wanted to see the place again!"

She sensed Ashley and Jason move behind her, using her body to shield themselves from the ranks of dark figures. Even Trent, still at her side, had taken a small step back. She sighed.

A ripple moved through the group of shadow children, as if they had all tilted their heads at the same time.

"We have nourished ourselves with the blood of those who would destroy us." One of the figures crept forward. "We wish to restore ourselves."

Ashley tugged at the back of Mindy's shirt and hissed into her ear, "We really need to leave, Mindy."

Mindy half-turned to her friends, still watching the creatures. "You guys get out of here while I've got them distracted," she said quietly. "Wait for me outside the Kiddie Town gates; I don't think they can go past the fence."

Trent and Ashley looked horrified, but Jason nodded and began backing away from Mindy, ushering the others along at his sides. When they were ten feet behind Mindy, she saw them turn and run. The train whistle piped again, stronger than before, and she tried to ignore it as she took a step toward the ranks of shadow figures.

"We are not here to harm Kiddie Town or anything in it," she said, slowly and clearly. "We love everything here as much as you do." Okay, she thought, that might have been a *slight* exaggeration. "We're going now. We won't bother you anymore."

She thought this might have confused the figures. A susurration ran through the group, harsh and incomprehensible as wind whirling through a stand of trees. Finally they fell silent and all turned their silvery eyes on her.

"It has been too long. We fade. We need you, that we might be strong again."

Mindy swallowed and nodded, inching backward. She had no idea how fast they were, or how much power they exerted. They were still several yards away from her, and if they really weren't strong yet, maybe she stood a chance. In a quick motion she spun around on one heel and jumped forward with her other foot, sprinting toward the front gates of Kiddie Town.

The kiddie coaster had traveled the full loop, and she narrowly missed suffering the same fate as Jason as she sped across the tracks. Up ahead were the miniature train tracks, and she whipped her head side to side looking for the Kiddie Town Train. It was nowhere in sight. She hoped that meant it had made its way to the opposite end of its loop and wasn't in a position to run her over. She barreled her way across the tracks and slammed into the fence, barely registering the horror-struck looks on her friends' faces as they grabbed her and helped haul her over. As she pulled her foot to safety, she thought she felt something wrap around her ankle, then slide off, wispy like shadows.

"Don't look back," Trent panted. Mindy didn't know if he was out of breath from running, or from fear.

The group limped and shuffled away from Kiddie Town, through the ruins of Joyland as quickly as they could, exhausted but desperate to leave the shadow creatures behind. As they made their way around the husk of the Scare Shack, just before Kiddie Town was lost to view, Mindy turned to look back.

Kiddie Town had gone dark once more, lost in shadow. But within those shadows, Mindy could still see pinpoint glints of silver reflected in the moonlight. The shadow children would wait for the next group of trespassers unwise enough to enter Kiddie Town, looking to recapture childhood dreams but finding nightmares instead.

CLICK-CLACK

T.S. WEAVER

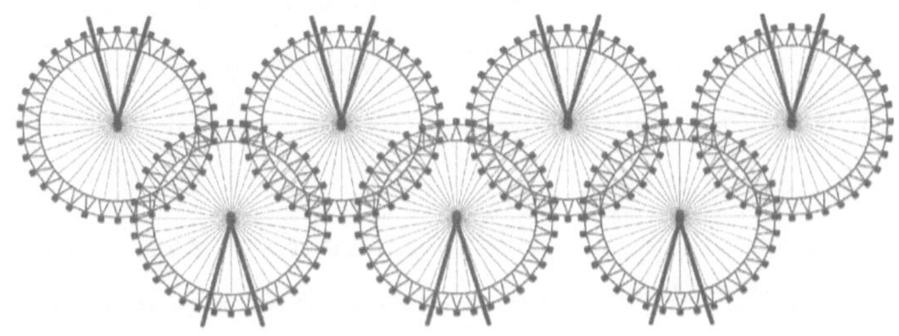

I MOVE WITH CARE from shadow to shadow, slipping through the darkness. This is my home; I know every part of it, all the shops, restaurants, cinemas, even down in the aquarium, but that doesn't mean I'm safe. I keep myself hidden whenever possible, moving through the open parts of the structure only when I'm certain I'm alone save for the hunters and the rats, mice, and other small creatures who avoided the click-clacks.

They won't find me. I won't become their prey. Yet my heart beats faster at the thought of being spotted. Fear tightens my chest, threatening to turn my guts liquid. My nose twitches and I take a deep breath, testing the air for their presence, my tail curled around my body.

I know the risks, what will happen to me if they catch me. I've seen it happen to others. I've stumbled across the remains, the bones with only the barest scraps of flesh still clinging to them, fur, hair, clothing. Shreds, nothing more. They waste nothing. Often the bones, when I find them, are cracked open, marrow gone. The only things safe have been those in the aquarium.

The click-clacks don't like salt water, but it didn't save the swimming ones. With no one to look after them, they all died. Some long before the first of the new hunters arrived. More than a few had become food for those who'd ventured into the once-busy place, searching for anything they could use to stay alive.

I won't go out that way. I have no real control over what happens to me when I'd dead, but I'll not become prey to one of those things. I am a hunter, terror of the teeth, death on four legs to those small furry ones who crawl and chew on cables. I will not fall to a click-clack.

It won't be just one.

No, they travel in packs. I rarely see one moving through the giant structure on their own. A scout might venture out from the group, but I always act as if there are more of them around. It's safer that way simply because it's true. They work together, they move as a unit, like the insects in summer, except they are bigger, and aren't insects.

They have some shared features, but the scent, sound, the thick oozing stuff that drips from their jaws only to bite into flesh, shares nothing with the small skittering ants, beetles, or other things that have always existed.

I dart from one shadow to the next, careful to remain soft pawed. Any sound that might draw the hunters my way is to be avoided.

It's quiet today and not for the first time I find myself missing the screams that used to echo through the central open part where so many rides waited for both young and old. Maybe that's strange, I don't know, I've given up trying to remember what was normal. That word no longer means the same thing. This normal, the one where silence is safer, where being alone is best, where the only companions are shadows and memories, yes, this is now what my mind tells me is normal.

I listen, muscles tight beneath my skin and I wait.

This had been a safe place.

I don't know what changed; I haven't left here since—well, I don't remember when or if I ever did. I don't know how long my home has been like this, only that it changed. I was brought here, I recall that, young, small enough to fit in the palm of one hand.

There had been others like me then, older, who'd taught me. Explained why I had been given this strange home with so many people around. Most were kind to us, feeding, petting, offering scritches, but others—I learned to avoid certain ones. Their scent often gave them away.

Once, just once, I want to hear something that doesn't send me running for cover. That used to be normal here. I'd sit out of the way and watch as the young ones ran from one ride to another, tickets in hand, or bands about their wrists. Sometimes adults followed them, dragged by the youngest in the group, others sat on benches watching or glued to screens.

Noise.

Always noise. Even at the end of the day, when the rides closed, and the people were gone, the background hum of energy moving through black cables remained. Most of the lights would be switched off, but some remained on through the night until the doors opened again, and everything returned to normal. But now even the hum is gone.

Laughter, giggles, yelps, shrieks, I miss them all but most of all it's the screams I find myself straining to hear, even though I know they, like the source of the noise, are long gone.

What screams I hear now aren't ones of delight, but fear, terror, and pain. There's little left here to draw the crowds, and the mingled laughter, screams, music, and footsteps no longer provide the background soundtrack for my life. Instead there is silence. Blessed silence and with it the knowledge I'm alone.

It's been a long time since I've had anyone to share this space with.

It's safer that way.

Others have tried to make this place their home, but they don't survive.

They make the mistake of trusting.

Metal scrapes against metal.

I freeze.

People?

A part of me hopes, but I know better.

You can't trust them. They will always betray you. Gentle hands, warm embraces, shared meals, those are all a thing of the past. If they reached for me now, I'd run. No matter the temptation. I couldn't risk being snatched up the way one of the older teachers had been.

One of the last of my companions.

Killed, stripped of fur, cooked over open flames in a storeroom, and eaten.

Hateful people.

What harm had she done to anyone? To them? She still caught mice, and the older rats, still did her job, the one we'd all been brought in to deal with. It hadn't mattered to her that the people had gone; she'd been taught to do this, we all had, and they had her loyalty.

They don't have mine.

Not anymore.

Dangerous, worse than the click-clacks because we'd once trusted them. They'd been our friends, family, protectors, but no longer. Not after the old one, leaving me alone.

The rest were gone. Dead or slipped out past the closed exits, through small gaps. Yes some of the doors were open, from the place where vehicles had sat, or doors left propped open by those who'd thought they could return in safety.

Yet I miss the noise.

It meant safety. Play. Children. Most of the time children had been safe.

Not anymore.

Then there were the things. The new creatures, the vile dark hunters. They'd come after the others had fled, when the voices fled, and the screams died only to be replaced by other noises. Still screams, but darker, filled with pain, horror, and sometimes, on rare occasions, defiance. I didn't want to hear them again, but they would return.

No more pleasure and joy, only pain, fear, and terror.

Something clatters, sharp-pointed sounds of feet moving across the floors. Claws, long, dangerous, and too many to count, skitter between the rides. My chest tightens and I turn, flattening myself to scoot under one of the rides. I wriggle, squirming my way between the cables until I am buried among the heavy black rippled snakes that hold the now-silent cables.

I don't want to see them; don't want to know they are back. Shutting my eyes helps me pretend they aren't there, but I can't shut out the sounds they make.

Clicks of feet, claws, the clatter of strange mouth parts as they open and close their biters. Not like birds, but also like birds. Beak like with sharp biters inside. Long tongues that snake out, snatching up anything they see as food. Even each other.

I hide in the darkness, among the dead snakes, that's the safest space. Small places, tight places, where they can't find me, but back, back away from the reach of their tongues. Wicked evil tongues. I shudder and keep my eyes open. I won't be caught by them. No biters allowed. Not in my body. I am not food. Hunter, not prey, but not like them, not ever like them.

"No!"

I can't move, don't want to move, everything locks in place. The word carried by a scream.

I don't want to hear. Don't want to know. Don't want...

A second scream. Not the same voice. Deeper, older, other emotions behind the sound. Fear for another, for the younger voice.

Sounds I don't want to hear, terror and pain torn from blood filled throats.

No.

They aren't here. Don't exist. I won't see. Won't hear. Won't taste. Not real.

Scrape, click, clatter, click click click.

More wet tearing.

Claws. So many claws.

I remember. Lights. Noises. Humming black snakes under the rides. Laughter.

Click. Click. Click. Clatter. Skitter. Click. Snap. Snap. Snap. Click.

Footsteps. Small, light, fast. Heavier ones follow.

Click-click-click. The claws, talons, tipped with death, follow the steps.

Other memories. Songs, there'd been so many different songs played by the rides. They merged, clashed, but somehow remained separate. Rocks songs, pop songs, different names and voices. I didn't know what they sang about most of the time but remembered a few of the words I'd learned.

My tail snaps back and forth, rubbing against the black snakes. I freeze. Movement makes noise. I can't be found, seen, heard, it is the only way to remain safe, to not become prey.

Rapid movement, a different set of footsteps.

My fur twitches and I wriggle backward, deeper into the black nest.

Screams. Ripping, tearing sounds, flesh and cloth. I open my mouth, tasting the air, drawing it across my tongue, and shudder. My stomach growls remind me to hunt later, to find one of the small rodents that avoided the larger prey. The same fast-moving furry ones who threatened the humming cables before the noise died.

My stomach clenches. I won't take the leavings of the creatures, not when they eat two-legged prey.

Click. Rip. Tear. Clatter. Click.

Claws.

So many claws and no more laps, soft beds, dishes of food, or praise for catching the small furry ones. The click-clacks changed that.

But they haven't caught me.

They'll never catch me.

I won't become prey...

JERICHO'S STAR

CHLOE YORK

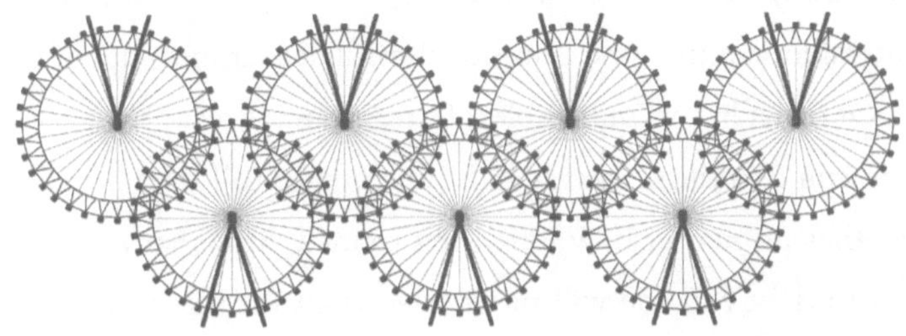

No one knows what happens in Dr. Jericho's act. The details of his exclusive performances have been kept secret since the Carnaval de Rêves began visiting Rowan's small town many years ago.

Some say Dr. Jericho makes his audience's most impossible wishes come true before their eyes. Rowan's heard others say it's a scandalous sex show. Her theories, she thinks, are the most inventive. Impossible rarities, mythical beasts, miraculous feats of magic—the kind she once believed in.

Out of habit, Rowan seeks out the familiar hand-painted sign, the one with the glinting dagger resting atop a mass of flowers, *Dr. Jericho* in flowing calligraphic text on top. *Invitation Only.*

She flicks through the pressing crowd, adjusting her glasses and smoothing back her hair, still damp from the shower. She was in there longer than she meant to be, jaws closed around her fist so her roommates wouldn't hear her sobbing. All around her, the carnival is alight with rainbow fire, a melody of delighted shrieks and laughter setting her teeth on edge.

She's always loved the carnival at night. The savory sweetness in the air, the calliope music, the communal thrills. It reminds her of simpler times. Of belief in the impossible, of dreams made real.

She's come to the Carnaval de Rêves tonight to forget her shattered goals—that no matter how long she's trained, how many classes she's gone into debt for, she will never have what it takes to make it as a professional singer. She has no stage presence. No charisma. She's not pretty enough. Not brave enough.

Not...enough.

Overcome, she halts between the carousel and a red-striped tent, every line of her rejection email clinging like syrup in her chest.

We regret to inform you that after carefully reviewing our judges' audition notes, we are unable to offer you a spot in our program.

As her eyes prickle with fresh tears, the roller coaster car whooshes by overhead with its screeching passengers. Inspired, she sucks in a long breath, mindless of the crowd, the game booths, everything.

When the cries build above her head, she adds her own to their chorus, a cleansing, delirious scream she summons from her most cavernous, hopeless depths. When it's over, she collapses against a light pole, face in her hands.

"You have a remarkable scream, young lady."

Rowan sucks in a hitching breath as she stands and twists toward the man cocking his head at her, his face half-obscured by the tent's shadow.

"I'm—so sorry," she stammers. "That was...loud."

The stranger sidesteps an overturned popcorn bucket, tipping his top hat to Rowan. He's dressed like an old-fashioned sideshow barker, his handsome tailored suit emphasizing the lithe form beneath. Affixed to his left pocket, a watch glints in the technicolor light. He presents her with a black-gloved hand to shake, spine straight, eyes crinkling at the corners.

"My name is Dr. Jericho," he says. "And you, little screamer?"

Rowan falters, backs up a step.

"You are not," she laughs, too star-struck to take his offered hand.

He straightens his top hat, grants her a theatrical bow.

"You've heard of me."

"Your show," Rowan clarifies, heat growing in her cheeks. "I mean, everyone has. I—"

"Have you been crying?"

She swipes beneath her glasses, granting him another shy giggle.

"I'm fine," she lies. "Bad day."

He leans in.

"May I ask why?"

Rowan considers. To start, she had no one to join her at the carnival tonight—she hasn't spoken to her parents in months, her friends all went away for college, and her roommates are at a frat party, one of many they neglected to invite Rowan to.

Her music consumes the entirety of her gray life, yet she's still turned down for every residency and performance, relegated to just another faceless voice in the chorus. Not the spotlight. Never the spotlight.

But here this man—Dr. Jericho himself!—is offering her comfort, an ear.

An attractive one.

For someone whose name has become the subject of many a campfire tale in Rowan's town, he looks young, not much older than she is. Her blush deepens. She presses a hand to her cheek to tamp it down.

"I kinda blew this audition the other day." Her gaze flicks to her feet. "I'm a singer. Or at least I want to be. Anyway, I got the email today. They don't want me. So." A forced smile. "Hence, the scream."

In a blink, he's beside her. Another and his gloved hand is atop her shoulder.

She trembles as their eyes lock. Up close, his are the rich brown of worn leather.

"How much do you know about my show?"

"I don't even know anyone who's seen it," she says around a swallow.

A meaningful pause.

"Would you like to be one of them?"

Her response comes after a stilted intake of breath.

"What?"

Dr. Jericho's hand trails the length of her back, soothing, patronly. She feels his touch in every molecule, every cell crying out for his proximity.

"And I don't mean for you to just watch. I've been considering adding an opening act to my show," he says with a slant of a smile. "Someone with a strong voice and the right..." He scans her. "Look."

She gapes at him, at a loss for words.

"Me?"

"You," he confirms, blonde brows raised, teeth flashing. "Only if you're interested, of course."

"Well, yes! I mean—"

Just then, her foot catches an errant tent stake. Before she can right her stance, she stumbles, arms extended to catch herself. She lands atop a jagged stone, scrapes her left palm on it. She shuffles upright, equal parts humiliated and exhilarated as Dr. Jericho lifts her up.

"Let me see," he says, holding her injured hand. Her breathing quickens with the contact.

"So embarrassing," she mumbles.

His pocket watch catches the red glint from the Ferris wheel as he holds it above her palm.

"Fortuitous, I'd say. Watch carefully."

Dazed, she obeys. He whispers over the watch, over her bleeding hand, where an odd tingle has taken hold. Reflexively, she jerks her hand back. Stops. Gasps.

The scuffed, raw scratch has vanished, as if it never was. She rubs the newly unmarked spot, beaming with involuntary delight.

"How did you do that?" she says, her voice bright, awestruck.

"I can do a great many things," he says. "So. What do you say? Would you join me tonight?"

She knows better. This sort of thing doesn't happen in real life. No one just puts you in their show without so much as an audition. Nothing is this easy. But still, she agrees.

How can she not?

"I knew you were magic," she muses aloud.

He chuckles at that while he guides her around the tent, the one they've been standing beside since she released her cleansing scream. *His* tent.

Wordlessly, he flicks his hand through the air as a magician might and what was once a solid vinyl wall opens before them. The first thing she discerns are flowers. Lush peonies, dew-flecked roses, and creeping ivy tumbling from marble urns. A hallway lined with...doors?

Rowan scans the tent's circumference from the outside. It can't be more than fifty feet in diameter. Large enough for a small crowd, but certainly not enough to accommodate multiple rooms.

With his hand on her lower back, they step into the cheerfully illumined tent, passing the fragrant blooms. She seeks a light source along the tent's peaked ceiling and grassy floor, but finds none.

"How is it so...big in here?" she asks when they stop in front of a richly lacquered door with a painted gold star on it. A dressing room.

"As you said," he grins. "Magic."

With another flourish of his arm, the door creaks inward and Rowan is presented with an enormous dressing room. Three racks of dresses, shoes, a three-mirrored vanity with an assortment of cosmetics and fine jewelry. The playground of a starlet, the type of woman Rowan has always longed to be.

"Wear anything you like," says Dr. Jericho. "The show begins in one hour."

"Wait," she falters, reality striking her all at once. She's about to perform. In front of people. No direction, no script. Her mouth goes dry, palms tingling. "What'll I be doing exactly?"

"You're a singer," he says, grazing her jawline with his gloved fingertips. "You'll sing."

"But...I don't—" Her patience is waning, nerves overtaking her. "How do you know I won't ruin your whole show?"

"I know your voice," he says. "And I know what an opportunity like this means to you. All you need is for someone to give you a chance. And if you do as well as I think you will, there could be a permanent place for you here. If you want it."

She stammers, chest hitching.

"You're offering me a job?"

"Contingent on your performance, yes."

Rowan seats herself before the vanity, her face stretching into the first true smile she's felt in weeks.

"You know, I never did get your name," says Dr. Jericho. "Or should I just call you Little Screamer?"

"It's Rowan," she says. "Rowan Adler."

"And what song will you be performing, Miss Adler?"

"*Think of Me*," she blurts. "From *Phantom*?"

"A lovely choice," he quips. "I'll have the music queued up for you."

Only after he's gone does she notice how silent everything is, like there's more than just vinyl tent siding separating her from the lively carnival outside.

"It's okay," she murmurs. "You can do this."

Breathing hard, elated like never before, Rowan selects a sleeveless black gown that ends above her knees. She pairs it with glittery gold heels—not too high, she doesn't need to trip—and at the vanity, she does what she can with her hair and makeup. Without her contacts, she has to lean in close to see what she's doing. When she's as confident in her appearance as she can be, she puts her glasses back on and does a cursory twirl in the full-length mirror, practicing her vocal exercises, getting her voice in tune for what's to come.

She's going to be in Dr. Jericho's show. This is really happening. And what's more, this could become her new life. Traveling with her beloved Carnaval as a real singer at *the* Dr. Jericho's side...

She continues to sing with her whole body, hand atop her diaphragm, inhale, exhale. When his knock comes, Rowan darts from her chair. Before she lets him in, she removes her glasses, setting them atop her folded clothes.

"You're a vision," Dr. Jericho says. His features are blurred without her glasses, but she knows he's smiling as he offers his arm. "Are you ready?"

"Yes," she lies, a knot pulsing in her stomach.

They stride arm in arm down a plush red carpet before emerging into an open ring surrounded by curved bleacher seating.

Dr. Jericho's audience studies them from behind simple black masks, the kind used in fencing. Immaculately dressed men and women. Without corrective lenses, she can't properly count how many there are, but that suits her just fine. She can pretend no one's watching, that it's only her and Dr. Jericho.

"Welcome, my esteemed guests," Dr. Jericho says, directing Rowan to a microphone before a rose-colored lounge straight out of a regency romance film. Beside the exquisite chaise is a low table covered by a velvety black cloth. Props for his mystery act? Like the hallway, the entire arena is flooded with flowers. She plants her trembling feet and inhales the florid, honeyed scent of them.

You can do this.

"It is my sincere pleasure to introduce Miss Rowan Adler in her debut performance at our Carnaval. Let's make her feel welcome."

The applause is immediate, jarring, and complete. Rowan can't keep from grinning as she adjusts the microphone. Dr. Jericho seats himself on the lounge chair behind her. Waves a gloved hand.

Without preamble, the music starts, carried by an invisible orchestra. With no time for second-guessing, she shoves her consuming doubts away, grasps the microphone, and *sings.*

It's as effortless as breathing. No faltering. No stumbling. Her greatest performance.

When the song concludes, she releases a startled yelp when the audience surges forward, their cheers a deafening uproar. All for her. She did that.

Tears gathering in the corners of her blurred vision, she laughs as Dr. Jericho winds his arms around her middle and nuzzles her neck with his nose. His presumptuous contact, while surprising, isn't unwelcome. She hopes he'll kiss her, do more than kiss her. This pure, utterly *magic* moment is the culmination of everything she's ever dared to wish for. She doesn't want it to end.

Until he drags her to the chaise and slams her onto the cushions. Until he takes hold of her wrists and binds them with rope, the knots quick, expert, unshakable.

The audience has joined them in the arena when he pins her ankles together and straps her to the lounge so she can't even rise, let alone run.

"What are you doing, stop, let me go!" she shouts in a single breath, struggling against the ropes until they rub burning welts into her wrists.

Dr. Jericho twists from her thrashing form to regard the audience.

"A rare talent, isn't she?" he says. "And yours to enjoy for one authentic, consequence-free evening. Of course, the standard rules apply. No undressing. No fatal blows. And cannibalization, while not prohibited, is strongly discouraged."

This gets several laughs from the encroaching audience as he turns toward the table beside the chaise and removes the black cloth to reveal an array of surgical tools, pliers, filigreed knives, delicate saws.

"Oh god, please no," she whispers, going for another desperate thrash, but his bindings are too tight, too expert. "*No.*"

Near her ear, Dr. Jericho says, "You sing beautifully. I am truly honored to have you here."

Rowan's stopped hearing him through the piercing ringing in her ears, her hummingbird heart fit to explode.

"Now, you'll all get your turn," announces Dr. Jericho as he lifts a scalpel. "But the inaugural cuts are mine."

"Please," Rowan tries. "Someone help me, please!"

A piercing sting erupts along her temple, ice and fire trailing her hairline. Clasping her face in one gloved hand, he carves into her scalp, down to the bone. Blood oozes from the cut as she screams. Oh, how she screams.

"Good, Rowan. Yes. That's perfect," he praises, his grip tightening, his blade pushing deeper. Then, in a quieter tone, "They're going to love you."

He lets go of her chin and crosses to her feet. In the struggle, she's kicked off one of her heels. Like a lover, deliberate and slow, he replaces the shoe.

The audience is buzzing as their hidden gazes rake over her, an electric murmur of approval for their new star.

When she's able to open her eyes again, Dr. Jericho's replaced the scalpel with his pocket watch. With a gentle smile, he whispers over it and all at once, she understands everything.

Like her scraped palm, he's healing her. In several tingling seconds, relief comes. The deep gash along her hairline closes. Fades until nothing's left but the drying blood caked to her brow.

This is Dr. Jericho's legendary attraction. This is what these people are here for. To hurt her. Over and over and over and—

Through her tear-soaked, fuzzy vision, their numbers seem to have grown. Twenty, thirty, she loses count. She will satiate every one of them tonight.

Dr. Jericho is close enough for her to catch his expression, bereft of emotion. His work is clinical. Impersonal. But deep in his eyes, there's something akin to pride. Righteousness.

"*Please*," she tries, suffocating on the overpowering floral musk buried under the coppery tang of blood.

The audience collectively shivers behind their masks, pleased by her fear. Dr. Jericho was right. They do love her.

With his scalpel in one hand and the pocket watch in the other, he leans over her and says, "Sing for us, little screamer."

With the knife, he carves into her shoulder blade and with the watch, he heals the gash. Then he turns to the audience, the motion punctuated by Rowan's lilting wail.

"Who would like to go next?" he asks.

Hours pass.

Rowan loses count of the cuts, the stabs, the flayed skin, the slowly sawed-off limbs, how many times they gouged her eyes and yanked out her teeth. If asked, she wouldn't be able to say exactly what was done to her. How much her body was forced to take beneath Dr. Jericho's magic little watch.

Yet how they praised her, adored her, *worshipped* her. How the admiration in Dr. Jericho's stare intensified as she received every one of his clients with increasing fervor in her melodious cries.

She is undeniable. Unforgettable.

His brightest star.

When it's over, when all their patrons have gone, the arena is saturated with crimson pools and scraps of forgotten viscera. Pieces of her embellish the floral arrangements. A foot here, a bouquet of fingers there. Her original earlobe—still adorned with its silver hoop—rests beside three of her molars, half-hidden beneath ribbons of bloody flesh.

Alone, Dr. Jericho undoes Rowan's bindings, pulls her into his arms, breathes into her sodden nest of hair. With a silken kerchief, he cleans her face. Eagerly, she nestles into him.

Remade, reborn, without a single flaw on her creamy skin, all that's left of her beautiful voice is a rasping, "*They loved me.*"

"As I knew they would," says Dr. Jericho. "You're remarkable. Just remarkable."

Swallowing, eyes drifting closed, Rowan drags his face to hers.

"Thank you," she whispers against his lips. "Thank you."

The Carnaval de Rêves slumbers. The gaming booths are shuttered, the rides skeletal silhouettes, all lights extinguished, silent as a tomb.

And from more than one sleepless mouth within Rowan's little town comes the whispered query, "What do you think happens in Dr. Jericho's act?"

Because—naturally—no one has ever seen it.

MR. RED

MARIE MCWILLIAMS

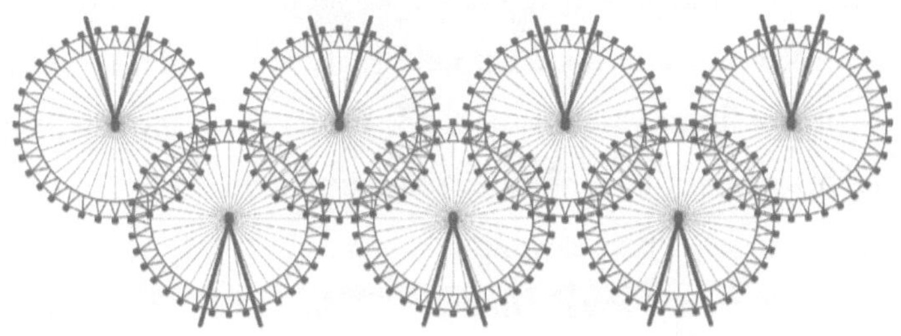

Patrick was the first to be taken. Small for his age, he was all puppy fat and awkward movements. We'd been playing at the creek, catching little fish and racing homemade boats. The others were swimming, splashing each other with cool water. I was nursing a cut when I noticed Patrick standing nearby, waving to someone at the distant tree line. The person was too far to make out clearly, but through the warm, hazy waves, I could just make out a tall figure, all dressed in red.

"Who ya waving at, Patrick?"

"The clown."

"The...clown?"

I moved my eyes back toward the trees, but the figure was gone. There had been nothing overtly untoward about it all, yet I found myself feeling unnerved.

"Come back over Patty. Let's look for minnows, eh?"

I remember steering him toward the creek, away from those trees, as if even at that distance we were too close to whoever, or whatever that figure had been. I kept glancing back, wary, but Patrick didn't seem to notice. We played all afternoon before daylight faded and the stern voices of our parents filtered across the field. We ran back most of the way together before splitting off for our respective homes.

That was the last time I saw him.

The next morning brought sirens and police cars. It didn't take long for word of Patrick's disappearance to spread. Patrick's brother had burst into an empty bedroom and an open window. The only clue was a big red plastic flower perched neatly on his pillow, the kind that squirts water.

I'll never forget his parents' faces. His mom's was tearful, collapsed under the weight of worry. But his dad's was ashen, sunken into a scowl, as if already resigned to the fact that Patrick wouldn't be found. At the time, it didn't register as strange, but later, when everything came out, I thought back to that day and I shuddered. There were search parties, flyers, appeals from cops and local media, but nothing was ever found of little Patrick Mackie, nothing but that damned red flower.

Slowly, the days grew shorter and the temperature fell. Us kids went back to school, painfully aware of a chair without its owner. Christmas came and went. My mom made me bring the Mackies a casserole once a month in a big tinfoil dish, a way of showing support without having to actually talk about it. I hated those visits. There was so much silence I felt the need to fill with inane chatter about anything except what I knew we were all thinking. My mom stopped sending the casseroles by Easter, an unspoken acceptance that Patrick was gone forever.

By the time summer rolled around again, the weight over the community had subsided. Children played in the streets again as parents worried less. But the peace didn't last long. Exactly one year after the disappearance of Patrick, Rachael Croft vanished.

The unspoken tension caused by the anniversary of Patrick's disappearance meant us kids stuck together a little closer than usual, just in case, yet we retired that night without incident. The next day was like déjà vu. Police swarmed the streets, and the phone never stopped ringing. "Oh no!" my mom would say over and over again, her mouth ajar, "it's just so awful." By the time I found out what was happening, a casserole was already in the oven, the egg timer slowly counting down the minutes that Rachael was gone. I wasn't allowed to join the searches this time; my mom determined to keep me close, safe. It had been exactly the same: a missing child, an empty bed, a red plastic flower.

Rachael's mom had died when she was a baby and her father was the only one left to cry for their missing daughter. He took it hard, crumbling under the weight of it all, crying constantly in great big noisy heaves we could hear over Father Maguire's tedious sermons. One missing child had raised the local news station, but two brought state-wide attention. A handful of camera crews stood in front of that field the first week, but disappeared after that, seduced elsewhere by a better story. As with Patrick's disappearance, the search parties went from daily, to weekly, before dwindling away. The posters of her yearbook picture, smile wide, pigtails neat, grew tatty and faded and the world moved on.

But it wasn't the same after that, and never would be. Parents were wary, children afraid. There was a boogieman in town, snatching kids and leaving behind a red calling card. The school developed a buddy system, and children were directed to walk home in packs. Parents put locks on their children's windows or nailed them shut, determined that it wouldn't happen again. But, of course it did.

His name was Ben Newcolm. Tall for his age, broad shouldered, big chested, he was the oldest to be taken at ten years old. I never much liked Ben. He was a bully. He picked on other kids, taking their lunch money, tripping them or smearing dog shit on their bike handlebars. He was big and dumb and I didn't have a good word to say about him. Still, I wouldn't have wished what happened on him.

Just like before, Ben went to sleep and seemingly vanished in the middle of the night. His dad had been on edge that night on account of the anniversary; we all were, the whole town holding its breath. He nailed Ben's window shut and sat by his bed, shotgun in hand, daring someone to come. But, at some point he must have drifted off. When he awoke, that window had been pried open, the nails protruding from the frame like teeth in an angry maw. In the place of his only child, he found the same plastic token, a single stain of red on faded bedding.

National news media swarmed, knocking doors, interviewing anyone they could. There were all sorts of police with different uniforms and acronyms for names. Town meetings were held at which angry residents blamed police, the mayor, immigrants, because anger is a useless emotion unless directed at someone or something. Cadaver dogs were brought in, sniffing and pawing at every ditch and hole. That's how they found the clown.

I was there that day, watching from the police tape as it danced on the breeze. The wood was not particularly big, but it was thick, the canopy of trees casting it in perpetual shadow. I remember the dog's insistent barking, its paws digging at the patch of dirt as its tail wagged happily. They put up a big white tent, the people coming and going busily in matching jumpsuits. Crowds gathered, gossip circulated. I hated what a spectacle it had become, as if it were entertainment, yet I found myself drawn there. It was the third day of digging when I saw the clown.

I didn't notice him at first, distracted by the repeated flash of a bulb within the tent. He stood further down to my right, just behind a group of whispering, grey-haired women. He wore red head to toe, a billowing jumpsuit made of shiny fabric, ending at his cuffs and collar in a frill. His oversized shoes were also red, as was the round nose in the middle of his face. He was bald, his head painted the same white as his face, with a wide red mouth painted in a frown.

I was confused, curious. Why was there a clown standing by the crime scene and more importantly, why was I the only one who seemed to find it odd? A travelling circus wasn't unusual in our part of the world. They would roll into the town every couple of years, seemingly popping up overnight and for a few days, everyone would be abuzz. I would visit with family and friends, watching the show in the big top while stuffing stale popcorn into my mouth, showing off my aim at the shooting gallery, or laughing at some love-struck teenage boy failing to win his sweetheart a stuffed animal. After having our fill of cotton candy and rigged games, the circus would disappear just as fast as it had come, leaving behind a trampled field and a few piles of garbage. But there was no circus in town that year. In fact, none had come through since the year before Patrick had disappeared. So where did this clown come from?

The more I mulled the question over, the madder I became. It seemed disrespectful to me, to stand beside what was most likely a grave, dressed like Bozo. I thought he was maybe driving through, using the influx of people in the area as some way to make a buck. I talked myself into saying something when I noticed it on his costume. I remember how cold I suddenly felt, despite the summer heat, and my hands shook. Tears filled my eyes as realisation dawned on me. Hadn't Patrick mentioned a clown? Hadn't I seen a figure, perhaps in this very spot, wearing red? I shuddered as I stared, fear flooding my mind. It was a flower. A big, red, plastic flower just like the ones the child snatcher had left in exchange for his victims, just like the one I had seen in the papers and on television.

He turned toward me and I froze, unable to move, my heart pounding. He fixed his eyes on mine and for one long, terrible moment, we just stared at one another. Then, he smiled, a big, wide, fake smile which slowly stretched across his face, cracking the white makeup as his lips curled back to reveal blood-stained teeth. Some teeth were cracked, missing or jagged. Blood seeped from his mouth, oozing down his chin.

I wanted to scream, but I couldn't seem to do anything except stand there slack jawed and shaking. I'm ashamed to say, I pissed myself, the warm liquid flowing quickly down my shaking legs. One of the old women noticed, came toward me with concerned eyes and dulcet tones. But I couldn't hear her, couldn't break eye contact with that clown. Only when one of the woman's friends briefly blocked my view of him was the spell broken. I didn't say a word, just turned and ran. I never told anyone what I saw that day, especially after I found out what had been buried there beneath that tent.

Inside an unmarked grave, police found the body of Chester Martin, aka Mr. Red the Clown. He had been a carny all his life, travelling town to town since he was a teenage runaway. He'd rolled into our little slice of America four years prior with a circus called The Red Top.

I never saw the body of course, but my friend Pauly, whose brother was a deputy, said that he was a skeleton by the time he was found, held together by dirt and blood-stained clothes. They had to use dental records to identify him. The circus folks had reported him missing, but the cops didn't take it seriously. After all, carnies were renowned nomads. They didn't seem concerned that Chester had left without his possessions nor did it raise any suspicions when they heard he'd gotten into an altercation with a local the night before he vanished. "He's moved on," they said, "you know what them people are like." But the circus folks took it seriously, packing up the very next day as if afraid more of their kind would vanish as well.

The sheriff stood at a podium addressing the press to announce that, while they hadn't made progress on the missing children, they had located a body. Somehow, the murder of this unfortunate soul was connected to the disappearances, though they were unsure how, but it wore a red, plastic flower identical to the type found in each of the children's bedrooms. I remember my face falling as they showed an old photo of Chester, appealing for witnesses to come forward. It couldn't have been him I saw; he had been dead, reduced to bones. Yet, it was him—I was sure of it, just as I was sure he'd been the one to take the children, although we wouldn't find out why until later.

Inquiries were conducted, leads followed. Old reports were dug out of storage and witnesses spoken to. Eventually the trail led to "Juke Box Joe's," the sleazier of the two bars in our town. That was around the time Mr. Croft stuck his hunting rifle under his chin and painted the walls with his blood. He left a note confessing everything, leading to the arrest of Stephen Mackie and eventually, after a five-hour armed standoff, Ben Newcolm, too. The three of them had murdered Chester, and that's why he had taken their children, that's why they'd been chosen.

Stephen Mackie's wife, Laurette, liked to drink and dance, so she would frequent Joe's most weekends. That fateful evening, there had been a few strangers at the bar drawing suspicious glances from the locals. They were from the circus, and Chester was among them. They kept to themselves, aware of the biases of small-minded mid-Americans, all except Chester. He must have liked the look of Laurette, and he asked her to dance. Laurette liked to make her husband jealous, so she said yes. Predictably, Stephen Mackie went for Chester, all puffed chest and angry threats. Joe, being a no bullshit kind of guy, told every one of them to get the hell out of his bar and that was the end of it, at least as far as everyone else was concerned.

But Stephen Mackie was drunk and angry and the fight was broken up before he got his fill. He and his two best friends, Ben Newcolm and Robert Croft, all hopped up on whiskey, made their way to the big red tent sitting on the edge of town. They found Chester sleeping and threw him in the trunk of Croft's car. One of them, none could remember exactly who, suggested ditching him in the woods. It was on the opposite end of town from where the circus had pitched, so Chester would have a nice long walk to get home. Another suggested they should steal his clothes, just to make it extra humiliating. But when they opened the trunk, Chester was ready.

He kicked out at Stephen's face, his nose bursting in a spray of blood. Chester tried to run, but Ben tackled him before he could get too far, landing a couple of hard fists to Chester's face. It was supposed to stop there; they had only wanted to scare him, to teach him a lesson about hitting on other men's wives.

But it got out of hand.

Angry and sore, Stephen stomped his boot down onto Chester's skull. Ben joined in, aiming for ribs, catching Chester's outstretched hands and cracking fingers beneath his heel. Robert shouted, pulling the men away, but they were seeing red. Before they knew what happened, Chester lay broken and still in a sticky mass of blood, his eyes wide and vacant.

All three sobered up quickly, the realization of what they'd done settling over them. Panic came, images of court rooms and jailhouses swimming in and out of view. It didn't take long for that to turn to scheming and plotting. They rationalized it between themselves, reassured each other. He was dead, there was nothing they could do. It was a terrible accident. But people wouldn't understand, they would be judged, imprisoned. Before they knew it, they were digging a grave. The last they saw of Chester was the red plastic flower as they slowly covered him with dirt.

The media loved it, painted it as a salacious tale of sex and revenge. No one ever found those kids and honestly, I don't think they ever will.

BE CAREFUL WHAT YOU WISH FOR

ANN O'MARA HEYWARD

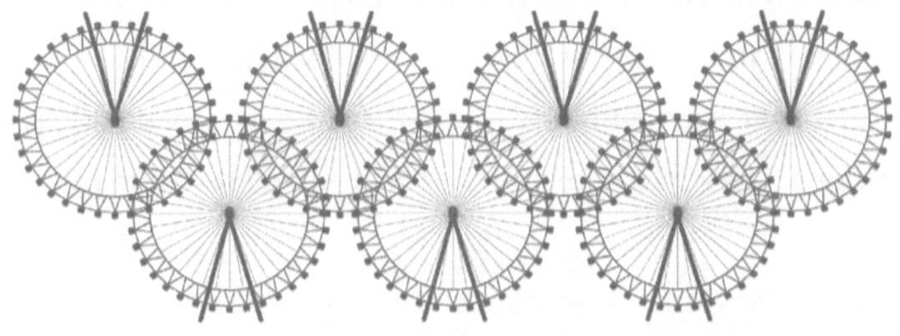

Around him, in the pines surrounding the fairground, birds moved halfheartedly from branch to branch, their cheeps and chirps and squawks muted, as if making a sound in the nailing heat took all the energy they had. He watched from the shade as his fellow carnies moved even more slowly, setting up rides and games and tents in a new town. Every town looked the same from the midway. But Jamie looked forward to the towns in Florida, more than anywhere else the carnival took him. The oppressive heat and humidity, even in October, felt like home to him.

And why not? He was a demon, after all.

At least, that was the only explanation that made sense to him. He had fought the strictures of his adoptive parents, good Christian souls who took him on as a baby who became a duty and finally a cross to bear. He had no idea who his birth mother or father really were. Always uneasy in church, when he turned thirteen it suddenly became unbearable. His skin itched and burned; his bowels cramped; his bladder felt as if it would explode. After the third beating with his father's belt for leaving their pew in the middle of the service and running outside to vomit into the grass, gagging and puking as if he'd never stop, he ran away.

On that long ago summer day, a carnival was in town. When it left that evening, Jamie Harris went with it as a gofer. He'd been a carny ever since.

The power to grant wishes also came to him as he went from boyhood to manhood. It had grown stronger with the passing years, but he still didn't entirely comprehend it. What made people so wishful in the first place? What made them wish for the very things they should not? They breathed their longings to Jamie, some hanging their heads in shame and self-loathing all the while. He did his best to understand what they *really* wanted, and to give it to them, but it always ended badly.

Not for him, mind you. He just moved on to the next town, and the next.

There had been that woman—Maureen—in the Midwest some-where. She wanted to be *seen*, to be no longer invisible in her mid-dle-agedness. He had lain with her, and she whispered her wish to him afterward. He had traced her tears across her cheekbones with a fingertip. He was gone before sunup with the rest of the carnival, leaving her be-hind sleeping in the campground grass, to awake that morning, changed forever by the elaborate script *look at me* tattooed across her face. Oh yes, Maureen would be seen, all right. As an oddity. Until her dying day.

Or the chester, Mitch, who'd joined the carnival in another forgotten town, a man who blinked too often and too hard, looking with naked longing at little girls passing by on the midway. Girls old enough to be at the carnival with friends instead of parents, but not old enough to have breasts that were more than buds. He confided to Jamie one evening as they passed a bottle back and forth at the carnies' campfire. *Wish I could have one of those cuties all to myself at the top of the Ferris wheel*, he whispered. *I could touch her and touch her and she couldn't do a damn thing about it unless she learned how to fly.* Jamie just stared into the fire and nodded.

The next day, Mitch broke his back falling twenty feet onto the generator for the Ferris wheel. He'd gotten on the ride with a twelve-year-old runaway. One smart enough to steal her stepfather's hunting knife when she left home, just in case she met someone like Mitch, and sent Mitch scrambling over the side of the car when she cut him, then slashed at his hands when he tried to hang on. Cuts were the least of his worries. Paralyzed from the chest down, Mitch could still yearn after tween girls, but that was *all* he could do.

Jamie had gotten a kick out of that one. The dark symmetry between wish and fulfillment amused him. It suggested larger forces at work. Long ago, he'd decided he was simply an instrument, a lure, for the pranks of some cosmic practical joker. With a mean streak a mile wide.

Who was the master Joker? Jamie didn't know and didn't care. He simply offered what he had; he never forced anyone. They accepted their granted wishes of their own free will.

He stepped out of the shade. The sun poured down on him like a molten blessing. He wondered whose wishes he would grant this time, in this town.

I'm sorry, the doctor said, *but you're no longer pregnant.* Dr. Anand delivered the bad news gently. Examination over, she laid her hand softly on Mandy's shoulder, then helped her sit up on the table.

That was a month ago. She'd gone to see Doctor Anand after the bleeding started.

Weeks before that day at the doctor's office, her period was late by a few days. She counted those days like beads on a worry bracelet as they slipped by, hardly daring to breathe. The days became a week, then two weeks, then three. She hadn't told Dave; he'd been let down so often. She didn't want him suffering the same swooning dive from happiness to grief again, when what they made was swept away in cramps and blood. And she dreaded the bitterness and envy tightening his face when he thought she wasn't looking, at the backyard barbecues and birthday parties of their friends, overrun with their kids.

This last time—for the first time—Mandy had done the drugstore test in secret, while Dave was out. She peed on the stick, then waited, eyes focused on her watch, not daring to look at the little window in the plastic wand as it sat on the corner of the sink. When enough time had passed, she'd tried to pick up the stick but her hands were shaking so badly that she dropped it on the floor, where it landed face down. *That's me all over*, she thought. She bent down, picked it up, and turned it over, bracing herself to see the single line in the window that would tell her *Not this time, kiddo.*

But there were two lines. Positive.

She had clutched the plastic stick to her heart in both hands. Then cried. Then splashed cold water on her face, dried off, put the stick in her skirt pocket, and left the house to go to the market. She slipped the test stick out of her pocket and into the wastebasket just outside the market entrance. *I'm sorry, baby,* she thought. *I'm just not ready for anyone to know about you yet. Until I know if you're going to be here for a while.*

The cramp hit her in the dairy aisle as she reached for some Greek yogurt. She stood, hands resting on the shopping cart handle, waiting, brought back to earth by an irritated *Excuse me* just behind her. *Oh please no. Not again. Not so soon.* She moved a few feet away, then left the cart standing there and headed for the door. She drove home, the cramps coming in waves now, fumbling her key at the lock in her haste to get to the bathroom. She slung her bag aside as she entered the front door, ran for the bathroom, and yanked down her underwear.

And saw the blood.

Jamie watched the cake eaters stroll by from his post beside the carousel, waiting to start his spiel again as the last batch of riders got off. His pitch was a meaningless singsong, *ride the tiger ride the one and only unicorn ride the pretty horses,* but it was never his words that drew them in. It was his aura that pulled at them. More often women, but men, too. The carnival boss used it to his advantage, putting Jamie out in front of any attraction lacking paying customers. Lorna, who sat in the ticket booth and sold her strips of colored paper to the sweaty masses, teased him about it.

Honey, she said, *you're like a porchlight on a house in the middle of nowhere. The moths will beat themselves senseless on you, they just can't help it.*

He liked Lorna. There was nothing she longed for. She was content with what she had.

Unlike the woman he saw now. She was part of a group of other thirty-ish women, who would still no doubt refer to themselves as girls, stopping to confer about where to go or what to eat next. He saw her head swivel as a couple walked by with a baby, who was banging their fat little hands on the stroller frame and bouncing up and down in excitement. The savage hunger on her face shocked him, and excited him. Even Mitch's perverse obsession was nowhere near as strong as this.

I think I have a customer.

The group of women, having made up their collective mind, strolled toward the carousel, laughing and tossing their hair, enjoying their all-girls good time. All except the one he'd noticed, trailing the rest of her friends.

Jamie took their tickets, one by one. When he got to the woman with the baby-hunger, he clasped her hand, holding her ticket, in both of his. She looked up, startled.

You should have what you want, he said, then let go of her hand.

She stared at him a moment longer, then followed her friends onto the ride.

Jamie started the carousel and hopped on as it began to spin, weaving his way between riders on their painted animals, until he found her, sitting sidesaddle on the horse she'd chosen.

The carousel organ thumped its percussive lilt around them. He looked up at her from near the horse's head, standing as if ready to lead the horse, with its damsel in distress, to some fairy tale place of rescue.

She looked down at him. She was weeping. He spoke to her, and she to him, shielded by the music from being overheard.

What do you want? More than anything?

A baby.

Why don't you have one?

I keep losing them. There's something wrong with me.

Maybe you're trying to grow something from bad seed.

She stared at him, thunderstruck. It was plain this had never even crossed her mind.

What would you do if I said I could give you a child?

She paused, looking away from him, hands clasped tightly around the pole, as her horse went up, then down, then she looked down and gave him her answer.

Anything.

Come back here after midnight.

She nodded.

He waited for her in the darkness, sitting on the edge of the carousel, listening to the crickets. He wasn't sure if she would come back. He told himself he was indifferent. She could take or leave what he was offering, of her own free will.

A pale shape emerged in the dimness. As she approached, he realized he was glad she had turned up, after all.

They didn't speak. There was no need. She stood before him and shed her clothes, without shame or coyness, sure in her purpose. The moon came out from behind a cloud and bathed her in blue and silver.

Surprised, Jamie shivered. The mother-goddess coming to take the seed of her consort was magic as old as life itself. Magic that didn't always end well for the giver of the seed.

He shrugged. He was, after all, just an instrument.

He dropped his t-shirt and jeans, watching her as he peeled them away from his skin. When he was naked, she stepped forward and put her arms around his neck. He kissed her. She tasted like honeysuckle when you chewed it on a hot summer day.

The night was warm, and they were both lightly sheened with sweat. Her breasts slipped and slid deliciously against his chest. He bent down and suckled her, and she gasped as his hand slid between her legs. She reached for him, closing her hand around his erection. She was wet; he was ready. It was time.

He lay back on the floor of the carousel; she straddled him, guiding him inside her warmth. He grabbed her waist with both hands, letting her ride him and set their rhythm, thrusting as she rolled her hips forward.

Her rhythm, and breath, quickened above him, as he arched to match her, meld with her, lose himself in her. Finally, she cried out. He came right after she did, a hoarse shout escaping him as he spurted inside her.

She rolled onto her back and lay beside him, then raised her legs and propped her feet up on the carousel's cheetah. She was holding her abdomen tightly in both hands.

Are you okay? What are you doing?

Holding it in. But it feels so hot inside me. It never has before.

I'm sorry. Did I hurt you? I didn't mean to.

No. It was good. It just feels strange, that's all. She smiled at him then. *Maybe that means this time will be different.*

They lay there without saying anything. At last, she got up, then dressed. Jamie lay and watched her. She looked at him for a long moment, then turned and walked away into the dark fairground. Finally, he couldn't see her any longer.

So good. Better than it had been for him in a long time.

He never let himself go without a safe, except tonight. Maybe that was it. He wanted no entanglements, and so far as he knew, even demons weren't immune to whatever diseases there might be. He'd been careful.

Maybe what felt so different was intention. He had *meant* to make something with her. A conscious decision on his part. Of his own free will.

So thinking, he fell asleep.

October again, and they were back on their swing through the South as the weather began to cool. That was the theory, anyway, even though daytime temperatures were in the nineties. As always, the heat suited Jamie just fine. He liked the slow pace of the carnival during the day, building up to its real life after nightfall.

And it was a pretty night coming, the setting sun painting a fire in the sky, like those paintings that were sold out of the trunks of cars by the Florida highways. Jamie could never remember whether the saying was *life imitates art* or *art imitates life.* Maybe both were true.

The boss would be happy with tonight's take. The carnival was crowded. Lorna, over in her booth, was all business, too busy to chat, tearing off strip after strip of ride tickets and scraping cash into her till as the next person in line stepped up. The bodies flowed along the midway in a steady flood, slowly around the circuit, like fish on a river bottom.

Jamie heard a distant shout, then raised voices. *A fight,* he thought. It happened. Somebody cut in line, somebody stepped on a kid's foot, somebody saw their ex with someone else. But the voices were rippling outward, growing louder. He stood on the carousel platform to get a better view. The boss might want the hands to break up the disturbance, whatever it was.

About fifty yards away, he saw the midway crowd peeling back from something moving through their midst. Someone walking forward through the crowd. He couldn't yet see them clearly. Whoever it was, people on either side were shrinking away from them like they had a contagious disease, and the raised voices didn't have an angry tone. More like shock.

Now he could see that it was a woman. As she neared, he saw a mother snatch her kid off the midway and turn away, hiding the child's face in her neck. One man crossed himself. Most turned their backs, and hastily stepped away, opening a path forward.

And no wonder, Jamie thought, *whoever she is, she looks like she's dying of fucking radiation sickness or something.* She was skeletally thin, walking in that wobbly way that famine victims did. A few sparse clumps of hair trailed from her peeling scalp. Her face and arms and legs were blistered, covered with what looked like cold sores running nightmarishly amok. Her clothes hung loosely on her body, ragged, dirty and bloodstained, as was the bundle she clasped in arms that were emaciated sticks.

She was looking directly at him. And grinning.

She laid the bundle at his feet on the floor of the carousel.

What do you want? he asked her.

Her shoulders began to shake and her mouth opened wide. At first he thought she was having some kind of seizure. Then he realized she was laughing.

And realized he'd asked this same woman the same question, a year ago.

You gave me what I wanted, she said. *Now I'm giving it back to you.*

She turned, and drifted away, the watching crowd closing behind her as she passed, murmuring softly.

Jamie looked down at the bundle of rags at his feet. It was moving.

He bent down and picked it up. The smell revolted him, but evoked a memory, so dim and distant it had to be from childhood. His childhood. Had *he* smelled that way, once?

Holding the bundle, he pulled back the rags to see what was inside.

It was a boy. His boy.

Who gazed up at him briefly, screwed up its tiny face, and began a discordant wail that sent the crowd away quickly, holding their ears against the pain, leaving him alone, holding this—this *thing.*

What the hell am I going to do with it?

He didn't know. He only knew one thing. This time, the joke was on him.

THE BLOWOFF

S.E. HOWARD

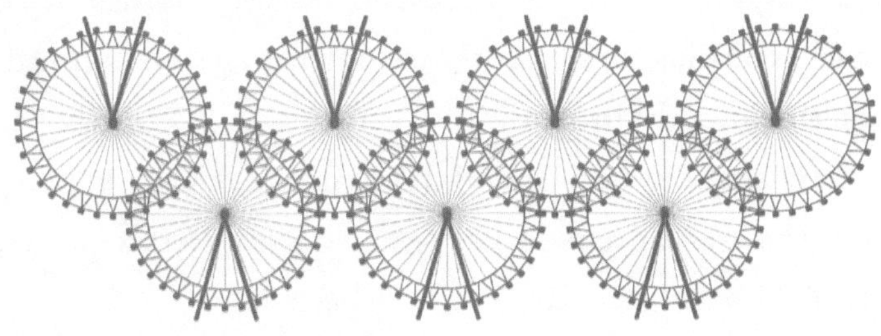

"I've got something you can swallow, honey," called a guy in a Lynyrd Skynyrd t-shirt, grabbing at the front of his Wranglers. I would have quipped something back to wipe the leer off his face, except I was distracted at that moment, trying to avoid perforating my esophagus—or worse—as I stood with my head craned back, the cross-guard on the hilt of a replica falchion resting less than an inch above my open mouth, the blade nestled down my throat.

I came from a distinguished line of sword swallowers, with my grandfather and mother both practicing the trade. While neither ever rose above the level of the same fleabag circuits I ran in, they shared a passion for the craft that my mother says I came by honestly. Despite this, she'd always discouraged me from following in the family footsteps, telling me time and again that nothing good ever came from the life of a carny.

Of course, she also liked to say I never listened, so it's no surprise that I'd become known as the Mistress of Blades, touring middle America as part of the "World-Famous Girls of Pandemonium." I didn't know about the "world-famous" part, but over the past year, we'd made a name for ourselves on the state fair circuit, and our manager, Gideon, had even bigger plans down the road.

"We're talking *America's Got Talent,*" he'd say, the lights of the big top flashing in his eyes like stars. "A Las Vegas residency, Netflix specials, and movies, like *The Greatest Showman,* only bigger!"

Gideon had all the sleazy charm of your average used car salesman. Every performer in his sideshow was female, and although we hated being referred to as "girls," he said that was our hook, what made us stand out from the competition. I suspected it was more of an ego thing for him than anything. Still, he managed to land the Girls of Pandemonium steady gigs in a business where if your performance schedule wasn't full, then neither was your belly, never mind your bank account, so as a rule, we didn't complain about it...much.

"How's the crowd tonight?" Ainsley asked as I ducked behind the side curtain. She went by the stage name Spitfire, and her bit consisted of bumping and grinding on stage to techno dance tracks while she spun and tossed flaming batons.

"Pretty good except for a pervy douchebag to the right of the stage," I warned.

"Thanks, Bea. I'll watch out for him."

Through a slim part in the drapes, I watched as she stepped out onto the stage, then picked up a plastic Bic to light her baton. The crowd ooh'd and ah'd at this, and as the lights came up, the music kicked in with a pounding drum beat, and she began to twirl in matching time.

"WHOOOOOooooo!" I heard the guy in the concert t-shirt yowl. "Baby, light my fire! Shake them titties!"

People like that were the reason my mother quit the business.

"In your grandpa's day, sideshow acts were treated like movie stars," she'd lamented. "By the time I started the circuit, shows were being bought out and shut down by bigger circuses that didn't want to fool with them. The ones that were left couldn't pull in the crowds. And the people they *could* get weren't worth a damn."

I'd asked her to teach me sword-swallowing and she said no. There was no future in it, she told me. My grandfather had still been alive, so I'd gone behind her back and asked him for help, to which he'd agreed. Upon learning of this—far too late to put a stop to it—Mom had simply shaken her head. "Oh, Beatrice," she'd said. "You never listen, do you?"

By the time I was eleven, I could knock back an eight-inch sai like a drunk with a shot of Jack Daniels. By thirteen, I was downing 12-inch tantos. At fifteen, I could swallow a twenty-four-inch rapier, then by seventeen, I could handle up to four at a time. At twenty-two, I was swallowing blades for a living, meager though it may be.

"Hey, Bea," Maxine said as I walked behind the big top and found her smoking a cigarette. She was up after Ainsley, and when she finished driving a six-inch nail through her left nostril, the twin contortionists Layla and Lila would wrap things up—literally, as well as figuratively.

"Hey, Max. You got an extra one of those?"

"Sure thing." She wore a shiny, form-fitting cat suit with thigh-high stiletto boots. Reaching beneath the top of one, she pulled out a rumpled pack of Camels and a lighter. "Here you go."

"Thanks."

"Looks like Gideon's going to introduce the blowoff tonight," she remarked, nodding across the field where we'd set up shop. On the far side of the weed-choked lot, just beyond the reach of the twinkling lights of the midway, I saw a lone tent, its vinyl panels black, with strings of red and white triangular flags stretched between the awning and the ground.

During the jump between our last gig and that one, Gideon had skipped out for several days. None of us knew where he'd gone or what he'd been up to, but upon his return, he said he'd secured what he called "a blowoff guaranteed to skyrocket our show into the stratosphere."

In carnival terms, a blowoff act is an optional encore. Audience members are given a teaser to entice them into paying extra to see it, but if they choose, they can "blow off" and leave. Gideon hadn't told us what the new blowoff was, and the only hints he'd offered had come during dress rehearsals, when he delivered his practice spiel.

It was bullshit, of course, some half-assed story about how he'd recently become acquainted with a gentleman from South America. This fellow, Juan Something-or-Another had confided to Gideon that he'd worked for a former high-ranking Nazi scientist who had moved to Argentina after World War II. Upon the scientist's death, he'd bequeathed to Juan a number of "grotesqueries," as Gideon called them—the results of experiments he'd brought when he fled Germany. Among those was something so horrifying and shocking it had to be seen to be believed.

"It's an abomination," Gideon declared. "A monstrosity born of the unnatural melding of DNA from two species never meant to combine."

He planned to sweeten the deal by warning patrons that anyone offended by nudity should refrain from taking up his invitation. Of course, this guaranteed most men in the audience would be in for a penny, in for a pound as the saying goes, and once the fees were collected, patrons would be directed to that mysterious black tent behind the big top.

As for those of us in the show, we were kept in the dark, with no idea what in the hell he had tucked away in there. Gideon had given us stern admonitions against snooping.

"It's dangerous," he told us. "You girls keep away. I catch any of you snooping, and I'll can your ass on the spot."

I wasn't sure whether to believe him. After all, Gideon was a showman by trade. He had a flare for the melodramatic.

"I saw them unloading something earlier." Maxine pointed toward the black tent, or rather, beside it, were a semi-truck was parked. The running lights were on, the engine still rumbling. "I heard a bunch of banging, too, like it was something big."

"What do you think it is?" Back in my grandpa's day, blowoffs would be silly things like "Giant Killer Rats of the Amazon"—which in reality had been capybaras or, less exotically, groundhogs—or "Spidora," a fake giant spider made out of fabric and wires, hanging on a goofy oversized web. Things like that wouldn't fly in this day and age.

"Don't know, but Gideon says it's going to make us famous," Max remarked, sounding as dubious of his theatrics as I felt.

"Yeah. Just like Hugh Jackman and Zendaya," I said and we both laughed.

She gave me another cigarette for the road, then said I could hang onto the lighter as she headed for her stage call. Once she was gone, I found my gaze again wandering toward the blowoff tent and semi-truck idling beside it. I didn't believe for a second that Gideon had brought back some top-secret Nazi experiment to use in the show—after all, nothing from World War II could still be alive and around today, certainly not working a part-time gig as a sideshow attraction. Still, I couldn't help but wonder. Why all the secrecy?

I thought about heading to the trailer used as our dressing room, but veered off course, stepping out of the pools of security lights and into the shadows. Maybe I'd meant to make my way toward that black tent all along. Maybe I hadn't, but either way, that's where I ended up.

I gave the truck a wide berth, sticking to the shadows as I approached, and could see the back doors of the trailer standing open, an unloading ramp still in place. I got close enough to notice a strange odor wafting out, one that reminded me of a possum that had been struck and killed by a car, bloated with rot, flies buzzing around the dull, clouded buttons of its eyes.

I crept toward the tent and leaned close, hearing nothing from inside. Glancing over my shoulder, I looked back at the big top. Maxine's act should be nearly over, the twins ready to go next. That meant Gideon would be getting ready, too, donning his signature red tuxedo coat and black top hat to play ringmaster.

I still have time then, I thought as I crouched down, lifting the bottom edge of the tarpaulin and ducking into the tent. *Enough for one peek at least.*

It was dark inside, the air muggy and stagnant, like the interior of a crypt that had been sealed for decades. I caught another faint whiff of rancid meat and in the blackness before me, I heard a faint scuttling, like tree branches dragging through dried leaves. After that, silence fell, as heavy and oppressive as the humidity. I still had the lighter Maxine had loaned me, and struck the flint wheel with my thumb. Sparks danced and sputtered, blinding me for a moment. It took another try, then a third before a flame burst to life.

A wavering orange glow spilled around me, and by it, I could see wooden benches arranged in neat rows. Beyond those, I saw the proscenium of a circus ring, a low barrier rising less than a foot off the ground.

It marked a central open space, but had been bisected by a heavy curtain separating the front of the tent from the back.

Still holding the lighter aloft, I crept past the benches. As I stepped into the ring, I caught a glimpse of movement: the bottom of the curtain swelling out gently, then sagging back again, as if rustled from the other side. I heard a quiet scrabble again, then the clink of metal against metal, like chain links jostling.

Something's back there, I thought, then realizing how idiotic and childlike this sounded, I shook my head. *Not something—some<u>one</u>.*

How much did I really know about Gideon anyway? He paid his workers on time, sure, and he kept us booked solid, but otherwise, not much.

What are you hiding? I thought. Even if it wasn't some sort of Nazi experiment, there was no telling what he could be keeping behind that drape. Had he done something illegal, gotten involved in human trafficking or drug smuggling? Something even worse?

I heard it again, that scraping sound, the jangle of chains. The lighter in my hand had grown uncomfortably hot, but I didn't dare put it out as I moved toward the curtain. "H-hello?" I called, low and shaky. "Is someone there?"

My voice faded as I drew aside the drape and saw what lay beyond. In my mind, I'd pictured awful things—animals chained up so they could be made to fight, or women and children stolen from somewhere else in the world, awaiting God only knows. Nothing in the darkest, wildest corners of my imagination, however, could have prepared me for what I found instead.

At first glance, it looked like a woman, with long, glossy black hair and a beautiful face, her skin as smooth, pale, and flawless as a bowl of fresh cream. Her eyes were dark, round, and glistened with reflected glow from the lighter as she regarded me. Her breasts were small and bare, her belly soft and flat, her waist gently narrowing. Beneath this, though, where her hips and legs should have been, instead was an insect-like thorax, a juncture from which eight spindly, articulated appendages protruded, each as big around as my forearm. Here was the scraping sound I'd heard—the tips of these scratching in the soft dust and straw bedding beneath her as she moved. .

A spider, I thought, realizing that's what she was, what I was looking at. Not some crude facsimile made from papier-mâché and pipe cleaners, this was real. Human flesh and form combined with a spider's.

"It's an abomination," Gideon's words echoed in my mind. *"A monstrosity born of the unnatural melding of DNA from two species never meant to combine."*

"Oh...oh, my God," I hiccupped, noticing something dark around her neck: an iron collar, with a length of heavy chain drooping to the ground, trailing off into the darkness.

Her mouth opened, and the fire glinted off a pair of black fangs, each as long as my hand. That was all I had the chance to see before I dropped the lighter, extinguishing the flame, recoiling in shrieking terror as she darted at me. In the darkness, I whirled to run away, but floundered into the heavy curtain, nearly dragging it down as I tried to claw my way past it. I felt her nails hook against my shirt as she grabbed me from behind, then sudden, searing pain as she sank those fangs between my shoulder and neck. There was a burning sensation as her venom hit, then what felt like a high-voltage electrical shock shuddered through me, and my cries choked short, all my muscles abruptly seizing. I crashed to the ground and lay there, mute and paralyzed, as a new sound filled my ears, low and hissing, like a ribbon of silk whipping across dry skin. Grabbing with her hands, prodding with her legs, she flipped me this way and that as webbing spewed from her spinnerets, wrapping my feet and working its way up, saving my head—my face—for last.

Oh, Beatrice, I could almost hear my mother saying, her disappointment obvious. *You never listen, do you?*

THE CAROUSEL

LAUREN MILLS

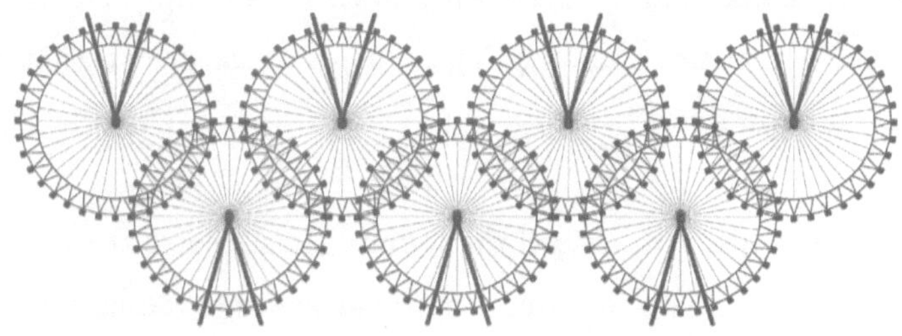

It was the sound that was missing. The familiar sound of the merry-go-round, screaming kids, creaky rides, and overpriced games. The smell of burnt popcorn and cheap hotdogs lingered in the air. The rides stood still, their neon lights flickering against the darkness. Reflected in the dim moonlight glow, the rides sat like skeletons in the desert. The tents zipped up and tucked away; the games, corpses in body bags. She drew the smoke into her lungs like a prayer.

"This fucking place," she muttered, "this fucking place."

She had packed up her portion ages ago. Everyone else had gone home to their families, but she stayed on. She knew she should leave, but the place had her hooked. In the hundred years since the carnival had rooted itself into the town of St. Augustine, no one had shown the fair more devotion than Josie. A uniquely American name for a distinctly

Australian seaside town, it sat perched next to a sea that instead of the usual warmth and draw of summer, was cold and unforgiving in winter.

And for the hundredth time that day, Josie thought of leaving. She looked at the rides and stalls. They had never felt so empty. Her ears still rang from a particularly unforgiving child. Josie flicked her cigarette and crushed it underfoot.

Josie...

She flicked her head toward the sound. Then smiled. It was the sea playing tricks on her. Taunting her. What was that old legend about sirens in the sea?

She started to walk away. But that's when she felt it. A tug on her pants.

Josie spun around; her paranoia met the cold empty air. She didn't realize she was holding her breath until she let it go.

"This fucking place..." she muttered again; this time the words rang hollow.

She went to move when she saw it at the corner of her eye. A kid, no more than seven or eight. Josie turned and took a better look. There was no mistaking, just beside the carousel was a little girl. Josie stood and waved at the little girl. She went to step forward but stopped. The girl's shadow seemed disjointed. And her smile was too wide. Then she giggled and ran behind the ride.

Dammit, Josie thought.

"Wait, kid!" she called, "it's dangerous around here!"

Josie ran after the kid, moving past the ride. She turned at the carousel and the girl was gone. Josie stood there scratching at her head.

"Hey kid!" she yelled. "Hey kid! Where are you? It's dangerous to be around here at night!"

She tried to keep her voice friendly and upbeat, but inside she was cursing. She did not want to stay at this place any longer than she had to. Josie cupped her mouth and yelled out again.

"Hey kid!" she yelled, "come on... let's both go home!"

Josie started to walk forward when the carousel came to life. Josie spun around, expecting to see the little girl on the ride. Instead, the ride seemingly reactivated itself. It spun, faster than Josie had ever seen it. Then faster and faster. Josie's stomach started to feel queasy. She walked over to it and looked at the plug. It was detached from the power source.

Josie stepped back and the ride stopped. A giggle flooded her ears, childlike and whimsical. But it faltered, twisted, turning into a deep low cackle that almost scraped along Josie's spine.

"Fuck this," Josie said as she sprung toward the exit.

She saw the exit, she could taste it, but as soon as she passed through—

She was at the fair again.

"What...?"

She turned; the air was silent. She walked through the exit—

Only to be dumped on the other side of the fair again.

"You can't go under it..."

"You can't go over it..."

The voices sung in a musical tone. It rang through her ears. She looked down the center of the fair. The little girl stood there, smiling.

The little girl, with the blue eyes and pale white skin.

Josie screamed as she ran around the corner. She maneuvered and jumped toward the tents. Hearing the pitter-patter of feet running after her, she wanted to scream but she held her palms over her face. Josie turned and dove into the haunted attraction. She felt her heart thumping as she closed the door.

And that's all she could hear. She tried not to breathe, hell, she tried not to think. She closed her eyes and just listened.

It's the booze, a frantic voice thought, *it's the booze getting to you! There was no little girl!*

There was silence. Josie took a breath, wondering if it had all been real. She shook her head.

No, not the drink, that little girl felt real. She closed her eyes and counted to ten. Then she listened.

And she heard nothing.

The silence was almost deafening. Shaking, Josie pushed the door open.

The darkness seemingly shattered against the sun's relentless blaze. She scrunched her eyes and looked around. No, not just the sun. The rides were there too. They all seemed to be moving. People gathered around them, laughing and clapping. Josie stood, slack jawed; had she been there all night? No. It was only a few moments. A second really. But here she was in the sunlight and the carnival was in all its glory.

Except it wasn't. It took a second for Josie to realize something was wrong, very wrong. She couldn't hear a thing.

"What the—" she said, then quickly clamped her mouth shut.

She lowered her hands from her face and spoke again.

"Hello?"

She couldn't hear it. The sound of the carnival. She stepped closer, into the middle of the circuit.

"Hello!" she called out.

She tried to grab a person passing by, but her hands went right through them. Josie stumbled backward onto the pavement.

"What..."

Josie stood up and looked around. She couldn't see the little girl, but the feeling was still there. It gripped her neck and held her close. She walked around waving her arms.

"Hello!" she called. "Can anyone see me?"

At first, she thought it was a joke. She went to the stand where they shot at the clowns, Mickey manning the station.

"Hello! Mick!" she said. "Hello! Hello!"

She tried waving in his face. She went to shake him but stopped. His grin was too wide; his limbs seemed almost disjointed. And the way he moved seemed almost mechanical. She went to touch him, but a cold hard fear gripped her.

Go on, touch him, a voice whispered in her head.

"Oh god," she said, "ohgodohgodohgod!"

Tears welled in her eyes and frustration swelled in her. She shook and doubled over. She wanted to scream, to holler, to do something, *anything,* to get it to stop.

This isn't real, a voice said, *this is all just a dream. You just need to wake up.*

Her heart hammered in her head. Shaking, she leaned against the pole, desperate for stability. For something solid in all this wrongness.

"Wake up," Josie muttered, "that's it— I just— I just need to wake up."

. That was it. It was all just a dream. The carousels, the games, their silence. It was unnatural, too unnatural. She started to walk, then run to the exit. She passed through guests and workers alike before she finally passed through the gate—

She was back at the carnival again. The noise, deafening in its silence. Josie screamed.

"It's all a dream!" she said. "This is—this is all a dream!"

She slapped herself in the face, but she felt nothing. Josie sobbed, collapsing to the floor.

But then she heard it. It was faint, but still there. She stood, almost bolted. And she heard it again.

Seagulls.

Seagulls by the pier.

Josie began to walk, away from the lights shining brightly on her face. Away from the crowds and the noise.

This is all a dream.

She stood, her back to the crowds, to the lights and the silence. She looked out onto the sea. The birds crying in the distance.

Josie pulled her body over the pier, her weight shifted, and she looked down into the ice-cold water. She felt herself teeter, then with the briefest hesitation, she fell over the side.

She crashed into the water, its coldness ripping through and piercing her skin. Twisting and holding her down tight. Josie wanted to reach out to swim but her arms were pulled back, held into place as though someone had tied a rock to her hands and feet as soon as she hit the water. She tried to hold her breath, but her body pushed for air. She gasped, water rushing into her lungs. Her eyes went hazy—she was faint—she was letting go—

And then she was awake. Shaking, just outside the haunted attraction. Josie fell to her knees. The people walked by and through her. Their smiles, wide and robotic. She placed her head in her hands.

"It's all a dream," Josie whispered, "it's all just a dream..."

Yes, a voice whispered, wrapping itself around her like smoke, *but can you wake up?*

EXILE

AMANDA M. BLAKE

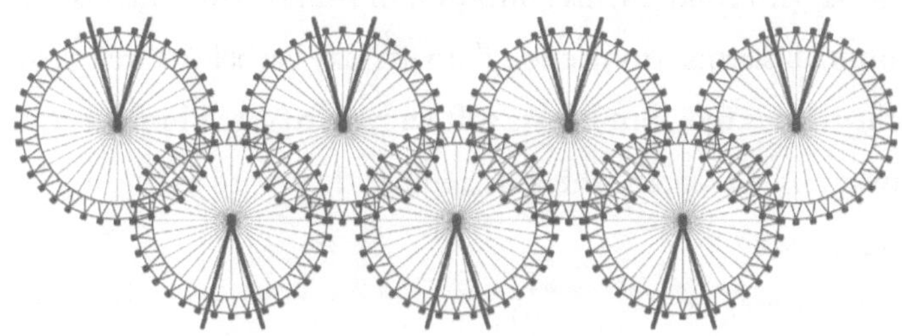

DUMPTY IS A GOOD clown. Gentle, funny, self-effacing, self-deprecating... Devoted to his profession, he's always ready to sacrifice himself for a laugh, be it through faceplant or pratfall.

But now, instead of treading earth strewn with sawdust, hay, popcorn, and peanut shells—wherever the trailer wheels took him—Dumpty tramps through leaf-spread forest. Any direction is as good as another after the ringmaster handed him his last few dollars of pay and told him he couldn't stay with the circus anymore.

Being a clown is a delicate thing, even when the clowns themselves are not delicate. So many children are afraid of them, but that's the antithesis of a true clown. Every clown who values his suspenders does everything they can to soothe a child who fears their great big grins and giant feet and exaggerated eyes like they fear the monster under their beds, with their great big grins and giant feet and exaggerated eyes, too.

Dumpty knows how to make an expertly tied-off balloon poodle or giraffe, he can whistle like a bird, and although his fingers are more cumbersome now, he can pull a quarter out of any kid's ear. He used to be so good with children, his rainbow jumpsuit billowy and his belly soft and round, his arms strong enough to lift fake barbells as well as some of the other circus folk, but his ass soft enough to catch him when he fell. He always used to make the kids smile if they were frowning, laugh if they were crying.

Not anymore.

He got his start with the Pickle-Dilly Circus as an already large clown, a teddy bear of a man with a chubby face, bald-headed as an egg.

But now Dumpty is a lumbering, looming giant. It doesn't matter how sweet he is when he casts a shadow as large as a barn, when children from infancy to puberty look up at him as though he'll fall on top of them, then eat them with syrup for breakfast.

Babies break into spontaneous sobs and will not be soothed until he leaves. Toddlers screech to shatter eardrums. Men who played basketball in college cower when he trembles the ground in their direction. Teens usually find it easy to mock the smaller, younger clowns, attempting to shake off childish coulrophobic jitters, but when he fills the frame of their view, their jibes fall uncharacteristically silent. No amount of gentleness can counteract the atavistic fear of every last guest when he crosses their path.

"You're just too big now, Dumpty. I'm sorry."

He slouches and staggers through the forest, searching for the widest spaces between trees so he doesn't get stuck. His feet, like red sleds, crush dead leaves, twigs, and young sprouts alike. Sometimes, he grabs handfuls of berries, fistfuls of leaves, and shoves them in his mouth. Not enough. Never enough. They just sicken him and make him hunger harder.

That's the other reason Dumpty no longer lives at the circus: He threatened to eat Pickle-Dilly out of house and home, consuming more than the strongman, lion tamer, acrobats, and tattooed lady combined. He raided the popcorn and cotton candy machines, the roasted peanut stash, the hot dog turners and the pretzel warmers, and of course the pickle barrels, outside as well as during working hours, to some guests' delight, at a distance—but certainly not to the vendors' or the ringmaster's.

If he walks far enough, he will stumble upon a fast-food restaurant or a gas station eventually, but he already ate through every previous paycheck almost as soon as the money changed hands from delicate white glove to oversized white mitt. He doubts the money burning a hole in his pocket will last long, and then what will he do?

It's still too hot to start looking for pop-up haunted houses that might take a good-natured clown and mold him in their image. They wouldn't even need to change his makeup—just find Dumpty a dark corner where he can unexpectedly stand and scare those who don't expect his bulbous head to be so far above theirs.

People who visit haunted houses *want* to be scared—or at the very least they *choose* to be scared—but he doesn't want to scare anyone. He just doesn't know what else to do with his giant feet, his white face, his big red smile, and his rainbow jumpsuit that can also satisfy the massive bulk of what's beneath all those things—the sheer size of him that makes moving feel like swimming through mud. And deeper, the never-ending hunger amid a roiling nausea—something in him gone horribly wrong.

The ringmaster knew it. The kids knew it. He knows it. But he doesn't know what to do about it. All he ever did and can do is be a clown. Now he can't even do that.

Dumpty walks until it gets dark. He's not afraid of the dark, but he can't see well enough to keep going.

Even though he's so hungry, so hungry—and yet so sick, so sick—he lowers himself next to a thicker trunk to lean against. Although a smiling clown should never cry in anything but paint, quarter-sized tears splash over his big red nose and grease-white cheeks to puddle on the ground.

Dumpty wakes hungrier than ever, but also even sicker.

Propped against the tree trunk, he wraps dead-log arms around his belly. He groans against the abdominal cramps that wrack through his churning viscera, lurching to and fro against the barrier of his external flesh, as though his insides strive to be outside.

He gags, retches, but whatever is within sticks in his craw, then withdraws once more, and he groans again, in too much pain and far too large to double over. All he can do is fall to the side, clutching himself as though to hold the entire bodily edifice together. He feels as though he's going to burst like a balloon animal confronted with a pin; perhaps that would be better than enduring each gut-wrench any longer, especially if he can no longer be what he is anymore.

Misery holds him down more than gravity, but what's painful inside him only becomes more insistent—like every case of food poisoning he's had the displeasure of cleaning from the bleachers, burning through him all at once.

His rainbow jumpsuit tears away like stretchmarks where his massive belly pushes against it. Lumps and bumps in the protuberance rise and fall, slow boil to the off-rhythm of cramps and roiling and rocking inside that leaves him dizzy, dimming.

Dark spots bloom ink spills in his vision as he stares up at the canopy, at the polka dots of light through the leaves. They're so pretty, and his stomach hurts so bad.

He misses the circus. He misses his bed. He misses safety and warmth and peace and people around him, the smells, the music, the laughter, the lights, like the lights in the trees, except these don't sparkle and there's no calliope, just his groans thundering through the forest. Even the birds have gone quiet.

He hears ripping again, but this time not from the shreds of his jumpsuit.

Dumpty bellows his loneliness, agony, and revulsion to the indifferent trees as his skin splits like a rotten pumpkin. He tries in vain to gather and hold himself in as his giant intestines spill to the sides, worms from the rot. But his arms have no more strength, *he* has no more strength, and the lights are fading, as though rewinding back into night.

But he's awake enough as the clowns exit their fleshy cocoon, climbing and tumbling out with lithe and flexible limbs, slender bodies, and the smooth, optimistic, red-smiled faces of youth, their generous curly hair springy and bright, their fingers deft in their gloves and their large shoes more like snowshoes than sleds.

One.

Two.

Three.

Four.

Five.

Six.

Seven.

Eight.

Nine.

Nine new clowns—each so different, but each looks so much like him when he began. Hard to imagine one belly could hold them all.

Deflated, Dumpty understands now. He's sad he can no longer twist balloon animals or make children laugh, but he's wearily happy that his inadvertent time of terrifying them is over.

His progeny will make so many children so much happier than he'd been able to these past several months. His rainbow-suited, white-painted, red-nosed legacy will continue.

Dumpty deteriorates quickly, his grinning head the last to collapse. His last image and thought is of the nine clowns as they all choose a direction and cartwheel joyfully away, while the obsolete clown carcass decomposes behind them.

ABOUT THE AUTHORS

AMANDA M. BLAKE

A mass of tentacles and rose vines masquerading as a person, Amanda M. Blake is the author of such horror titles as QUESTION NOT MY SALT, DEEP DOWN, and OUT OF CURIOSITY AND HUNGER, dark poetry collection DEAD ENDS, and the Thorns fairy tale mash-up series. For more, visit amandamblake.com.

MARIE MCWILLIAMS

Marie McWilliams is a horror author whose work includes *Mother Mort's Carnival of souls*, a novella accompanying an immersive Oracle deck and her debut novel *Broken Mirrors*. Her newest novel *The Secrets of Blackthorn House* is set to be published summer of 2025. Her short stories have been published in over a dozen anthologies and magazines and she has had multiple notable collaborations with various accomplished artists and book subscription boxes. When not writing or reading, she talks about her love of books and horror on her various social media platforms, primarily Instagram. Marie lives in Northern Ireland with her young daughter, who wishes she wrote about more pleasant things or occasionally wear colour, her partner, who loves everything she does and is her biggest cheerleader, and finally their small, one eyed dog, who has no opinion on the matter. Find out more at www.mariemcwilliams.com

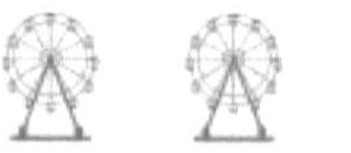

T.S. WEAVER

Originally from England, T.S. Weaver lives in Minnesota with her husband and her now-retired service dog. Her work includes military sci-fi, horror, and paranormal alt-history, with *Silverfur*, a post-apocalyptic novel in the same setting as Click Clack, releasing in March 2025.

CHLOE YORK

Chloe York, an award-winning abstract painter, insect taxidermist, and owner of a small oddities company, resides in Birmingham, Alabama with her sculptor husband and ferocious daughter in their shared home and studio. When she's not painting seascapes or framing bugs, she can be found in her lair writing fantasy and horror novels. Find out more at www.chloe-york.com

S.E. HOWARD

S.E. Howard grew up in the heart of the Bluegrass state, and has worked as a newspaper reporter, travel writer, and magazine editor. Her horror short story, "You've Been Saved" was adapted for film in the 2022 independently produced anthology Worst Laid Plans by GenreBlast Films. Other horror titles include the western horror novella "Prairie Madness" with Unveiling Nightmares, and forthcoming novel-length debuts "The Vessel" and "What Lies Unseen" with Wicked House Publishing. Currently a registered nurse, she is also a Certified Specialist in Poison Information. Find out more at www.sehoward.com

JAMIE CHURCHMAN

Jamie (she/her) lives in Kansas with her husband and an assortment of animal friends. She's been a weird little horror gremlin as far back as she can remember, and has been writing stories to scare others for nearly that long. Like the characters in "Kiddie Town," she also longs for the days of her youth at the real-life Joyland.

LAUREN MILLS

Librarian by day, writer by night and Eldritch horror between the hours of 4am-5am. Lauren has smattered their dark creations across the world, in the hopes of spreading terror, confusion and hopelessness where they can. If no one stops them, they are looking to unleash a terror far bigger than previous iterations next year. You can find them in dark caves, your nightmares, or on their website www.lrmills.com

ANN O'MARA HEYWARD

Ann O'Mara Heyward is a horror fiction and nonfiction writer in Cleveland, Ohio. Her short story "The Carny" won The Ghost Story's Supernatural Fiction Award (Spring 2023) and was nominated for a Pushcart Prize. Her fiction has appeared in Solar Press Horror Vol. 1, Jane Nightshade's Serial Encounters (Hellbound Books), GASPS edited by Judith Sonnet, Stories to Take to Your Grave, Mortuary Edition (Undertaker Books), Behind the Shadows II (Inkd Publishing), parABnormal Magazine, and been aired by the NoSleep Podcast. She is also at work on a nonfiction book "The Thinking Woman's Guide to Horror Movies." Find out more at annoheyward.com

LEONARDO LAMANNA

Leonardo Lamanna is an Italian archaeologist with a deep love for reading and writing speculative fiction. Whether set in the Paleolithic era, an urban jungle, an alien planet, or a post-apocalyptic future, his stories explore Homo sapiens' relationship with life and death. When he's not writing, he spends his time studying ancient, dusty bones, wandering through the woods, or playing with his three-year-old son.

D.L. WINCHESTER

D.L. Winchester lives in the foothills of southern Appalachia. A former mortician, his work searches the darkness to find tales worth telling. He is the author of over three hundred obituaries, numerous short stories, the story collection Shadows of Appalachia, and the flash fiction collection A Terrible Place. In his spare time, he can be found searching for inspiration in the world around him and trying to keep his children from becoming the next generation of horror villains.

If you are a fan of horror stories and tales,
you'll want to follow Undertaker Books.
We're bringing you stories to take to your grave.

www.ingramcontent.com/pod-product-compliance
Lightning Source LLC
Chambersburg PA
CBHW020045310726

48970CB00007B/2424